Forever My Love

Pride, Oregon Series
Book 15

Jill Sanders

DIGITAL ISBN: 978-1-945100-93-2

PRINT ISBN:

Copyeditor: Erica Ellis–inkdeepediting.com

Summary

Reece, destined for boxing greatness, takes an unexpected hit when a newcomer in his small town knocks him off his feet—this time, not in the ring, but in matters of the heart. Hailey, with her unwavering determination and air of mystery, becomes the unexpected force that reshapes Reece's world.

Hailey, along with her sister, seeks refuge in a new town, yearning to escape the shadows of their dark history. The sisters, bound by secrets, aim to rewrite their narrative. For Hailey, the small town becomes a haven where she finally discovers a sense of belonging and home.

Little do they know a sinister figure shadows Hailey, threatening to disrupt the fragile peace she's found.

In a twist of fate, Reece offers more than just boxing lessons; he becomes Hailey's defender against the darkness. As they grapple with secrets from Hailey's haunting past, Reece introduces her to the empowering world of self-defense, weaving a tale of resilience and newfound strength.

As trust and vulnerability become the battleground, Hailey finds solace in Reece's arms, and the two embark on a heart-warming journey of love and ambition. Join Reece and Hailey as they navigate the intricate dance between their shared pasts and their promising future in this captivating tale of resilience and passion.

Prologue

"Harper, wait up!" Fourteen-year-old Hailey Davis rushed after her sister, Harper. She knew full well there was no way she could catch her. Harper's legs were a lot longer and her older sister was better at running than Hailey was.

When Harper finally did stop in the middle of the field that sat somewhere between their home and the stream that the sisters spent most of their time at, Hailey was finally able to catch up.

"Are you okay?" Hailey asked, seeing the red marks on Harper's face from their mother's slaps.

"Sure, no biggie," Harper said, lifting her chin to the sky and closing her eyes as the warm Georgia wind blew over them.

Hailey wasn't surprised that her sister's eyes were dry. Harper never cried. Like, never.

When Hailey got slapped or hit, she always cried. Always.

"Your lip is bleeding." Hailey reached up and wiped her

sister's lip. Harper brushed her sleeve across her lip and then smiled down at her.

"Hey, I'll bet you anything that we caught some fish in our trap." She smiled, the cut on her lip opening a little more. "Wanna go see? We can grill it over a fire."

The thought of food made Hailey's stomach growl loudly. They'd gotten out of school a few hours earlier. The only thing Hailey had eaten that day was a banana and some milk that the school had given her out of obligation. She'd used up all of the weekly lunch coupons that the school gave her and Harper two days before.

It was the last day of school for the year, and she knew that there wouldn't be any food in the house for the next few months during summer break. There never was. Their mother didn't really eat. They never went shopping for food. Instead, their mother traded all of the food that she'd bought with the SNAP card the government gave her for drugs.

Most weekends, the only thing they had to eat were some apples from a few trees near the stream and any fish that the sisters caught in the homemade traps they'd learned how to build with sticks and string.

"Sure." She smiled and took her sister's hand as they strolled towards the stream.

She didn't know what had caused their mother to slap Harper that day, but the sad truth was that it didn't really matter. There were always reasons.

She'd once been smacked halfway across the room for stepping on a piece of trash, which had made a crinkling sound. She'd bumped her head on the floor and had burst into tears. Her mother had jumped on her and held her down, slapping her until Harper shoved her off. They'd run to the stream and had hid until after dark.

She couldn't remember a day in her life not being afraid of the woman who was supposed to care for them. The only one in her life who really did care was Harper.

Hailey knew that Harper was the stronger of the two of them. Not only did she never cry, but sometimes she fought back. At least against their mother.

That night, when they returned home, was the first time that Fred Leeroy spent the night at their house. Fred was their mother's drug dealer. He'd been coming around the house for a few weeks, usually leaving sometime before dark.

That night, everything changed. That night, Harper and Hailey learned there were things far worse than dealing with a drug-addicted mother. That night, they learned that there was nothing in the world to protect them from the real monsters.

Chapter One

"Hit me with everything you've got," Reece Crawford said, using his shoulder to hold the large black punching bag firmly. "Take everything you've ever been angry about and use it. See if you can knock me down."

Hailey thought back to that night a little over six years before. The fear. The guilt. The anger at herself for being so naive, so weak. She felt all of her muscles bunch up and respond.

She let loose a solid punch, and Reece took a step back and smiled at her.

"That's it." He chuckled. "Again."

She threw another punch, then another. She didn't stop until she was breathless and a sheen of sweat covered her skin.

"I knew you had fight in you," Reece said, dropping his hold on the punching bag.

Reece was by far the nicest man she'd ever met. Not that she'd met many nice men in her twenty-one years. As a matter of fact, she hadn't met any nice men until she and Harper had moved to the small town of Pride, Oregon.

Until that point a little over a year ago, when they'd driven into town and moved into their great-uncle's cabin, Hailey had loathed men. Hated even looking at them.

She'd never had a single crush on a boy in school. Never felt her heart flutter at the thought of her first kiss. Never really felt anything for boys.

Then Reece Crawford had walked into Baked, the pizzeria where Hailey had gotten a job a week after they moved to Pride, and something had awoken in her.

Something Hailey hated. Loathed. Feared.

At first, she'd avoided Reece. Until she couldn't.

The man came into Baked daily. Daily!

He spent most of his time sitting in a booth and working on his computer while sipping a soda and nibbling on bread sticks. Other times he was in there with his family or friends.

His sister, Hannah, had recently gotten engaged to Wyatt Auston, the new owner of O'Neil's Grocery store, the only grocery store in the small town. Hannah worked at Hidden Cove, the new neighborhood that sat just outside of the small town.

Hailey really liked Hannah. She had even gone on a few trips to the mall with her and her best friend, Avery Auston.

Reece's parents, Luke and Amber, were some of the nicest people that Hailey had ever met. Actually, everyone in Pride was nice, with the exception of a few high school kids that came in and left huge messes for her to clean up. Had she ever been that rude when she was younger?

Reece looked a lot like his father. He was well over six feet tall, had dark hair that he kept cut short, and had a beard, like most guys in town. She supposed it was an Oregon thing, to keep them warm or something. But the one thing that set him apart was his kind caramel-colored eyes.

Those eyes haunted her dreams. They made her think of things that she didn't quite understand. Things that she hated herself for thinking and dreaming. Things that made her think of the darkest night of her life.

"I think that's enough for tonight," Reece said, rolling his shoulders.

Hailey watched the move and when he glanced up and saw her eyes glued on him, she turned her gaze away quickly. She felt her face heat.

She'd never really been embarrassed around a man before. About the only real emotion she'd ever felt around a man was fear.

"How's your sister doing?" Reece asked.

"Good." Hailey walked over and picked up her gym bag. "She tore our shower apart. She and Nick are there right now, rebuilding our entire bathroom."

Reece frowned. "Do they need any help?"

"I don't think so. When I left, they appeared to have everything under control. Besides, the bathroom isn't big enough for another person." She sighed as she remembered that she'd need to use the bathroom at the Boys and Girls Club to shower for the next few days.

And she was going to need those showers. Reece had agreed to work with her every night this week to teach her self-defense and boxing.

When he'd first offered, she'd denied him. She didn't care about boxing and didn't need to know self-defense. She and Harper had never really gotten into sports.

But then she and Hailey had a talk the other night. Harper was afraid that the news report about her and Nick saving a busload of students during a bad snowstorm had gone national. The report told the world where they were and even where Harper worked, and her sister was seriously concerned that Fred would see the report and come after them.

Nick had used his connections as a police officer to find out that their mother had overdosed six years before.

For six years, the sisters had believed that Harper had been the cause of the woman's demise. Six long years of the sisters hiding from the world. Hiding from the truth. Running from the darkness they believed was after them.

Now, it appeared, the darkness might just catch up with them.

Harper had immediately suggested that they leave Pride. Hide again by bouncing from job to job, hotel to hotel once more.

To hell with that.

Hailey was done running. Done hiding. Done being weak. She no longer wanted to be someone who could be easily manipulated or hurt.

So the next time Reece had offered to train her, she'd accepted.

Everyone in the small town said that Reece was the best boxer in the state. She'd never seen him hit anything other than the punching bag, nor had she ever witnessed an actual boxing match, so she had nothing to compare him to.

"I was going to head to Baked for some dinner after. Do you want to join me after showering?" Reece asked.

She thought about heading back to the cabin. What if Harper and Nick were still there?

It was obvious to her that her sister and the cop were sleeping together. Considering their past, the knowledge that her sister was intimate with him made her uneasy.

After what they'd been through, she couldn't imagine letting a man get that close.

"Sure, why not. I'm probably better off avoiding the mess back home." She disappeared into the women's locker rooms.

As she showered off, she thought about her past. The things she'd been through, the things Harper had been through. They hadn't come out of their childhood unscathed. Hailey had tiny scars where their mother had burned her or cut her with a flying glass or beer bottle. But on the inside, it was obvious that Harper was more scarred than she was. And whatever pain their mother had inflicted on them, Fred had tripled it in just the year he'd been in their lives.

She took a look in the mirror as she combed through her hair. Since that night a little over six years before, she'd kept it styled shorter. One time the sun had lightened a few strands and she'd liked the look, so she'd started highlighting it herself. She'd never been to a beauty salon, even now.

It had taken her a few tries to get it just right. She'd done as much studying about hair products as she could on her phone or the library computer.

The couple years they'd been on the road, when she should have been studying for her GED, she'd taken a few online cosmetology classes instead. Even if she hadn't been trained in person, she knew everything there was to know about hair.

Whenever she had free time, she watched training videos or scoured through the latest products.

While Harper had her camera and photographs to fill her vacant time, Hailey had cosmetology.

Unlike her sister, whose hair and clothing styles were a little boring, Harper spent every dime that she had left over each month on stylish clothes and accessories. She adored Classy and Sassy, the boutique in town that was run by cousins Lilly and Riley.

Whenever she went in, she would spend hours talking to the ladies and looking over the new clothes. The cousins were each married to one of the twins who owned Baked, where Hailey worked. They both had kids and, even though Hailey had never really thought about having kids of her own, she adored Aurora and Benjamin.

It took her a while to figure out which kid belonged to whom because the cousins talked about both kids equally.

Benjamin belonged to Lilly and Corey, while Aurora belonged to Riley and Carter.

At first it was hard to tell Corey and Carter apart. The twins confused a lot of people in town. But after working with them for over a year now, she could easily tell them apart.

Corey had lighter hair and manned the pizza ovens while Carter, the darker-haired twin, ran the business side of Baked. He hired, fired, and paid employees, ordered supplies, and ensured that the bills were paid.

Hailey had been intrigued by how a business was run, and she'd enrolled in a few online business classes.

When Carter had found out about this, he'd kind of taken her under his wing. Whenever she had a question about running a business, he answered her and then made a point to show her how to implement what they had talked about.

Shortly afterward, Riley and Lilly started talking to her about how they ran their business as well. No doubt Carter had told them about her interest.

Hailey found it all so fascinating. But since she didn't want to be a burden, she kept her questions to a minimum.

When she stepped out of the locker room, she was surprised to see Reece sitting outside on a bench, already showered and changed.

His short, dark hair was still damp. He'd changed out of his sweats and was wearing blue jeans, tan hiking boots, and a green flannel shirt that he wore often.

He looked like a mountain man, the kind that should have an axe thrown over his shoulder. Still, her heart did a little skip at just seeing him. She felt an inner tension spike.

She hated what her body did around him. Hated that she couldn't seem to control it or her mind when he looked at her and smiled his sexy crooked smile.

"Ready?" he asked, standing up.

"Sure." She tried not to think about how he towered over her.

Many men did. That didn't make them Fred. That didn't mean they'd hurt her.

The Boys and Girls Club in Pride was far enough away from the center of town that she'd driven the old truck she'd purchased shortly after getting her job at Baked.

When they stepped outside, she pulled on the hood of her jacket against the rain, and they sprinted toward their own vehicles.

Reece drove one of those big trucks that most guys in town did. She knew it helped him get everywhere when the weather turned to ice and snow. Even her old truck was better in the snow than Harper's little car.

When she pulled into the parking lot of Baked, Reece parked right beside her.

Before she could gather her purse, he rushed over and opened her door while holding an umbrella out for her.

"Thanks," she said.

Their bodies were so close that she held her breath for a

split second. He smelled like spring showers, and she could feel the heat radiating from his body. When he took a step back, she relaxed and then followed him to the front door.

"Do you want a whole pie or just a slice?" Reece asked her.

"We can split a pie. You pick the toppings. I love them all." She shook a few drops of rain from her coat.

Reece nodded quickly, and they made their way to the cash register at the back of the restaurant to order. Carter was working. Her boss smiled at them when they stepped up to order.

"Can't stay away from this place, huh?" Carter joked.

She chuckled. "Best pizza in town."

"We're the only pizza in town," he pointed out with a laugh. "How did Hailey do in the ring?" he asked Reece.

Reece glanced down at her and winked. "I'm too afraid to put her in the ring. For now, she's bruising my ego by hitting the bags harder than I can."

"She may be small, but I'm sure she'd whoop your ass." Carter laughed.

After they ordered, she picked a booth to sit in and shot her sister a text message.

"Want me to bring home some pizza?" she asked.

"Sure, we're almost done for the day," Harper replied. "Another hour should do it."

"See you then." She tucked her phone back in her purse.

The sisters had agreed to be in constant communication with one another. Ever since Harper's image had been shared nationally, they were on guard.

"Everything okay?" Reece asked, sitting down across from her with a full glass of soda he'd just filled at the machines.

"Yeah, it looks like they're almost done for the night." She took a sip of her sweet tea.

"You're lucky Nick is helping. He redid his house a while back. You should see his shower." He shook his head. "I'm trying to fix up my own place now. Tile work is an art."

Reece had mentioned several times now that he'd purchased a place overlooking the town. The way he talked about it, there was a lot of work still needed on the home.

She thought about all the work that she and Harper had done the first few months they'd moved into the cabin, just to make it livable. The place had sat empty for a long time before they'd moved in.

Now it was home, the first one either of them had felt truly safe in. She would be damned if she was going to let anyone take that away from her.

Chapter Two

Keep your cool, Reece kept telling himself as he sat across from Hailey.

How long had it been since he'd first seen her? That moment, a little over a year before, when he'd walked into Baked and had seen the pretty brunette, he'd felt as if he'd been punched in the gut. Winded.

She was, well, a dream.

He'd danced around asking her out because he'd seen how jumpy she was around men that gave her attention. She seemed scared. Hurt. Leery.

So as to not scare her off, he'd bided his time, wearing her down by being friendly and keeping the flirting to a minimum. He was trying to convince her that he wasn't a threat.

For the first few months after the sisters had arrived, the entire town had talked about them. It had been obvious to everyone that they were running from something. Even Hailey's older sister Harper, who worked as a bartender at the Golden Oar, steered clear of men.

But recently it had become obvious that Harper and

Nick were an item, and Reece felt that it was time to try and break down a few more of Hailey's barriers.

When he'd offered to give Hailey self-defense lessons, he'd been sincere in wanting to teach her to stand up for herself against any threats. He was a firm believer that women should know how to defend themselves. A while back, his big sister Hannah had taken down a crazy woman who had locked her fiancé, Wyatt, in a freezer.

Hannah and Reece had both attended self-defense classes when they'd been children. After that incident, he trusted that his sister could handle anything.

Reece had enjoyed the classes so much as a kid that he'd joined a few other classes. He had earned a black belt in both judo and tae kwon do. Then he'd discovered boxing, which was his favorite sport by far.

When he'd been in high school, he'd entered a couple of boxing matches. Before he knew it, he'd won so many fights that his father had to build a whole trophy shelf for him.

In the past few years, money had started pouring in from the fights, and he'd been able to save enough to finally purchase a house. Even though it was rundown and needed a lot of work, it was all his.

After high school, he'd believed at first that he wanted to go to college. Instead, he'd taken a job programming and coding games with his father's company, something he'd done for as long as he could remember. The job allowed him the time to pursue his love of boxing while still paying the bills.

No matter the jock label he'd been given in school, he was a shy nerd through and through.

The freedom the coding job gave him to work when and where he wanted allowed him to spend more time with Hailey. He could take his work laptop anywhere and shift around town each day. He used to sit in the Brew-Ha-Ha bookstore, Sarah's Nook Bakery, or the Golden Oar restaurant.

Now his favorite place to work was in a booth in the back of Baked. This way, he got to chat with Hailey every now and then.

He'd never struggled to flirt with a woman before, though the last girlfriend he'd had had been months before he'd seen Hailey for the first time. It had been a very long, very dry year for him. Still, he was oddly satisfied with their interactions, even if they were just casual and friendly. But he did secretly hope for something more. Dreamed of what she'd taste like, feel like, look like underneath him.

"So, you can tell me the truth," Hailey said, leaning slightly towards him.

"The truth?" he asked, his eyebrows going up as thoughts of her under him—sated, warm, vibrating from his touch—played in his mind.

"How'd I really do today? I mean, I punch like a kid, right?" she said with a grin.

He smiled back. "You're slightly better than my sister, and she took down a stalker," he pointed out.

Hailey's eyes narrowed, as if she didn't believe him. Then she asked, "How did you get into boxing in the first place?"

"I was bullied as a kid," he answered truthfully.

She laughed, then dropped her smile when she realized he was telling the truth.

"I used to be really skinny and short." He shrugged and then took another sip of his drink.

"You?" She shook her head. "I don't believe it."

He chuckled, then pulled out his cell phone. His screen showed him at age ten with his favorite dog, Dutch.

Hailey's eyes ran over the image and then grew large. "Wow, you were really skinny."

"It didn't help that I was basically a wild child. I hardly ever stood still for more than five minutes," he admitted. "I ate everything in sight, or so my parents keep telling me, but just didn't gain weight. Until I picked up boxing."

"Who bullied you?" she asked, leaning back.

"Her name was Rebecca," he said, making her laugh again.

"Oh, you're serious?" she asked with a smile.

He nodded. "Found out in high school that Beckie, as she now likes to be called, had a serious crush on me at the time."

"Of course she did." Hailey sighed and glanced around, and he saw the spark in her eyes fade slightly. "I really like this place."

He frowned. She was talking like she was going to miss it. As if she had no choice but to leave. He fought the urge to ask her if she was staying, but that was stupid. She hadn't mentioned leaving.

"It's better with you in it," he said, kicking himself for not coming up with something better.

This time, instead of turning away from him or changing the subject, she ran her eyes over his face.

"Why do you do that?" she asked him.

"What?" he responded, not understanding her question. Was she asking him why he flirted with her or why he tried to compliment her?

"Why do you hang around here so much?" she asked.

His initial instinct was to joke about it. Then he decided to tell her the truth.

"Because you're here," he said simply. "Because there's

something between us that I'd like to explore. If you're willing."

She was quiet for so long that he wondered if she was going to respond at all.

"I've never... I haven't... I don't know what to say." She finally threw up her hands and leaned back in the booth.

"You never what?" he asked, curious. Again, she was silent. "Had someone interested in you? Went on a date? Had a boyfriend?"

"All of it," she admitted. "Any of it."

He was stunned into silence.

"Now I'm embarrassed." She buried her face in her hands.

"Don't be." He reached over and took her hands in his. He wanted to tell her it was okay, that he understood, but still, the questions flooded his mind. Why not? What had really happened to her and her sister that Hailey was twenty-one and had never gone on a date before?

Then he realized that he'd thought of tonight as a sort of date and immediately felt as if he'd cheated her somehow. If she hadn't ever gone out on a date, then he could at least show her what dating really was supposed to be like.

"How about we start over?" He smiled. "Hailey, I'd like to take you out on a date." He thought quickly. "How about this Friday evening?"

She frowned at him. "I have work."

He leaned back as Carter delivered their pizza and chatted with Hailey for a moment.

She went from tense to relaxed in a heartbeat as she joked with her boss. Then Carter left, and as they each grabbed a slice, she asked, "What about this?"

"This?" he said between bites.

"Isn't this sort of... like a date?"

He shrugged. "If you've never been out on a date, then when I take you out officially, I want to make sure you know it's a date and not question it."

She smiled. "Okay."

"Okay?"

"Sure, you can take me out on a date. I don't know when yet, but I'll let you know."

"Okay," he said with a smile.

He relaxed and, for the next hour, they enjoyed their meal and joked about her boxing skills.

He hated it when they finished the meal and she hinted at needing to get home.

As he walked her out to her car, he thought about when he would be able to take her out on a real date. About waiting until then to kiss her.

But as she leaned against her truck door, with the moonlight overhead occasionally being blocked out by the clouds, he felt that if he didn't kiss her now, he'd lose his chance.

"Thanks for teaching me self-defense." She shifted her bag on her shoulder. "The moves you showed me were really cool. Not to mention the boxing." She smiled.

"I like teaching you. You're a fast learner." He took a small step towards her.

Her eyes moved to his lips, and his gaze dipped down to hers for a split second.

"We still on for tomorrow night?" she asked. "It's going to be helpful to get out of the house since it appears Nick is going to be there again, working on the shower."

"I can pick you up after you get off work?" He leaned closer. "Maybe we can discuss our date."

She smiled. "What does one do on a date? Besides eat, I mean."

He smiled and leaned on the car door next to her, inches from touching her.

"Sure, food is usually part of it. We could go and see a movie. Or do a little shopping at the mall. Take a long walk on the beach or even a hike." He rattled off a few things that he'd done on dates before. Then he stopped. "Of course, the evening would end with a kiss." Her eyes once again darted to his mouth. When he looked at hers, he realized she was frowning.

"I don't like kisses," she said, shocking him.

"You don't?" He frowned. She shook her head. Then he smiled. "Maybe you just haven't been kissed by someone who knows how to do it right."

She was quiet and then shrugged. "Maybe."

His smile grew. "Do you want me to try and see if you like it?"

She swallowed slowly and then nodded. "We could try."

Hadn't he wanted this? To taste her, see what her lips felt like against his? Suddenly, a rush of nerves washed over him.

Without touching her, he leaned closer. He paused for just a second as his lips hovered over hers. Then he kissed her and his mind shut completely off. He let his desire for her take over his actions.

When he finally pulled back, he was breathless and a little dizzy from the powerful punch her kiss held.

"Wow," Hailey said softly.

"I take it you've changed your mind about kissing?" he said, feeling his own *wow* vibrate in his mind.

She nodded and then shook her head. "I... have to go." She ducked around him and opened her truck door.

"What time do you want to meet tomorrow?" he asked before she could shut the door.

"Seven."

He stood back while she drove away in the light rain. By the time he pulled into his own driveway, the rain had started coming down faster. There were even a few flashes of lightning in the sky as he stepped into the empty house.

The six-thousand-square-foot home had four bedrooms and four bathrooms. It had been built back in the early nineteen hundreds and had needed a lot of work before he'd finally been able to move in.

His dad and a few friends had helped him to basically gut the place. He'd updated everything—electric, plumbing, drywall, flooring, lighting—right down to the last door handles. It had taken five long years to get to that point. There were still a few spots that needed work, but nothing that had kept him from moving in. He'd fixed all the holes in the flooring and walls. Everything that was left to do on the home was cosmetic.

That first night, however, he'd realized just how lonely living alone was. He supposed it was the main reason he'd gotten a dog again.

The day after officially moving into his new home, he'd walked into Baked for lunch and had met Hailey for the first time. His entire outlook on life had changed in a heartbeat.

Chapter Three

Hailey loved her job. Even though most people would consider taking orders and delivering drinks and pizzas to be boring, she always had fun.

There were people to talk to, kids to entertain, and always stories and gossip to listen to.

She loved Pride. Loved almost every single person in the small town.

Sure, there were a handful of men who tried to flirt with her that she steered clear of. Obnoxious men who couldn't take no for an answer. The kind that always tried to grab her or, when she told them no, made fun of her by asking if she was a lesbian or a nun.

But after a few months of living in town, she knew how to avoid those types. Plus, Corey and Carter always stood up for her and kicked anyone out who was being too crazed.

Since Nick and Harper were spending the day working on the shower, she was thankful she had work to focus on.

When Nick's sister, Kate, came in and ordered her standard salad, she chatted with her for a few moments.

Out of everyone in town, she considered Kate, Avery, and Hannah to be her closest friends. Whenever one of them came in, she'd take her break and sit with them and catch up.

She had even gone on a few shopping trips to Edgeview with the group.

Kate ran her own dance studio, and Hannah worked as a real estate agent for Hidden Cove neighborhood. And Avery? Well, Avery did it all. She had jobs at the firehouse as an emergency dispatcher, filled in at Baked, Sarah's Nook, The Brew-Ha-Ha, and the Golden Oar restaurant, and sometimes worked down at city hall.

Everyone in town joked that Avery was a woman-of-all-trades.

Hailey respected Avery a lot. Not because she was unwilling to settle on a job but because she did all of those jobs to help others. The woman was the most selfless woman Hailey knew.

Avery and Hannah were BFFs. Apparently, when Kate moved back into town, the trio were once again reunited and were often seen together.

Hailey had never had any friends growing up besides Harper, so it was wonderful when the trio started including her in their activities. Whenever she'd suggest to Harper that she join in the fun, her sister either had to work or was working on the cabin.

Hailey liked the old place. Really. It was nice. The nicest place they'd ever stayed in their entire lives. Still, it was just a place.

Harper and Hailey both viewed the cabin as home. Even though Hailey liked the place, she knew her sister loved it. The cabin was more Harper's than Hailey's.

Her sister spent a lot of time and money fixing the home

up. Her sister's photos, which she'd taken with an old camera she'd found, were hanging on all of the walls.

Hailey didn't know if she had a style she liked for her living space, but her sister's style was everywhere you looked in the cabin. The fact that Harper was redoing the bathroom without Hailey's input didn't bother her.

"Hey." She sat across from Kate and set the salad down in front of her friend.

"Hey." Kate smiled over at her. "So, how was your first match with Reece?"

While Kate ate her salad, Hailey filled her in on her progress. She wanted to tell her friend about the kiss Reece had given her but was too embarrassed and didn't know if that crossed some kind of friend line.

Instead, she told her how they were meeting again that evening.

They chatted until Hailey's break was over, and then she got back to work while Kate headed back out in the rain. After two more hours of work, she headed home.

She had a couple hours before she was going to meet Reece for their next session and really wanted to see the progress on the bathroom.

After greeting both dogs, Lucy and Blue, she headed down the hallway and caught the last part of a conversation between Nick and her sister.

"I'm here," Nick said to Harper. "I'm not going anywhere."

Hailey froze as the couple sat on the floor in a loving embrace. Hailey didn't know how her sister could be so casual with sex. Not after...

She straightened and pushed the past behind her.

"Wow, this looks amazing," Hailey said from the doorway, causing the pair to jump away from one another.

"Thanks, we're not done yet," Nick said with a smile. "But at least you can now brush your teeth in your own sinks." He bent under the sink while she stepped inside. Somehow, the bathroom looked larger than it had before. Instead of one small sink without a countertop, there were two sinks, each with their own drawers, and plenty of countertop space for curling irons, blow dryers, and makeup.

Seeing her sister's red eyes, Hailey walked over and wrapped her arms around her. She knew when her sister needed a hug, and this was obviously one of those times.

"This looks great," she whispered into Harper's ear. Then she glanced over at Nick. "Thank you. I had no idea it could look like this," she said before letting Harper go to walk through the new shower area.

"We're going to start tiling tomorrow," Harper added. "Here are the tiles we picked out." She held up the tiles and Hailey could imagine how wonderful they'd look in the new shower area.

She knew that Harper was desperately trying to make it feel like a real home.

For the next half hour, Hailey let Harper rattle on about everything she had planned for the space.

Hailey changed into a worn pair of jeans and a T-shirt and helped them for a while.

While Nick worked on the plumbing, she and Harper started painting the new walls they had built with a soft cream color that Harper had picked out.

"This is the last thing I can do tonight," Nick said. "I'm going to head out. I'll be back in the morning and we can start on the tile."

"How long will that take?" Hailey asked. "I'm dying for a shower in this." She tapped the new shower wall.

"About two more days. You can shower on the third day."

Hailey surprised him and herself by walking over and giving the man a hug. Just knowing that Nick was there for Harper in a way that she couldn't be warmed her. Not once in the time they'd been in Pride had she feared the man. He hadn't even tried to flirt with her once. He was a cop and they had been raised to fear the police, but Nick was different. Nick was... good. "Thanks," she told him and then, pulling away, added, "Really."

Nick nodded and then Harper walked him and his dog out.

"Are you okay?" she asked Harper when she returned.

Harper nodded. "I think he knows."

Hailey's eyebrows shot up. "Knows what?"

Harper shook her head. "I don't know, but I think he knows... everything."

"What exactly did you say?" Hailey held her breath. If it was true, then Harper would likely force them to bug out. Each of them had bags already packed with cash and clothing, just in case they had to leave. They had agreed to meet at a spot an hour away, on the beach, if they ever got separated. If they had to run.

Just the thought of leaving Pride, of leaving Reece, had her heart breaking into sharp pieces that stung her entire body.

Harper shook her head. "I don't know. I mean, he mentioned something about how he'd be willing to kill to protect his family." Her eyes moved up to Hailey's, and she felt her eyes burn at the memory. "And I said I would kill to protect you."

Hailey took a deep breath. "Okay, then it's not so bad."

"No, it's... I think he understood. The way he looked at

me. I know that he understood what I was saying." Harper wrapped her arms around herself.

"Do we have to go?" Hailey asked between clenched teeth.

Harper shrugged, and Hailey knew that if it was up to her sister, they'd leave. Leave all of her new friends, her job, Reece.

"No, I won't go," Hailey said suddenly. "I'm done running."

Harper glanced down at her shoes. "Even if there's a chance we could be separated?"

Hailey rushed to wrap her arms around her sister. "They can never separate us," she said as the tears rolled down her cheeks. "Never."

Harper cried on her shoulder. "I won't let them take you away from me."

The sound of her sister crying for the first time she could remember shocked her.

"I'm not going anywhere." She repeated the words she'd heard Nick say when she'd come upon them and suddenly understood what he was telling her sister. "And neither is Nick." She leaned back. "He trusts you. I don't think... I don't think he's going to turn you in." She cupped her sister's face. "I think we can trust him."

"What if we can't? What if—" Harper started.

"I don't care," Hailey broke in. "I'm done running." She lifted her head. "Now"—she glanced at her watch—"I've got to get ready for my next session with Reece. You should come," she said suddenly. "Maybe we can learn something that will help us feel more secure."

Harper looked as if she were going to agree, but at the last moment, she shook her head. "No, you go. I'll finish painting in here." She hugged her again.

By the time Hailey stood on the mat across from Reece, she was even more determined not to leave Pride.

"Punch it," Reece said, holding the punching mitt up. She hit it halfheartedly with her closed fist.

Reece dropped his hand and looked at her, tilting his head slightly. "What was that?"

"I hit it," she pointed out, feeling frustrated.

Reece shook his head. "I know two-year-olds who can hit harder than that. Try again." He held up the mitt again. This time, she tried to hit it harder, but he dropped it again.

"You've been crying," he said, taking a step closer. "Want to tell me why?"

"No." She motioned for him to lift the mitt again. When he did, she hit it.

"Was it work?" he asked.

"No," she said, hitting the glove again.

"Did you have a fight with Harper?"

"No." She hit the mitt again, this time a little harder. "What makes you think I've been crying?" She hit the mitt again.

"Your eyes are red. And you're punching like a two-year-old. I know you have more fight in you." He lifted the gloves a little higher.

"My eyes are not red." She put more effort behind her hits.

Reece's lips twitched slightly, and she hit the mitt again with double the strength.

"Yes, they are." He ran his eyes over her face. "They're puffy too."

She narrowed her eyes and put everything she could behind the next punch. Reece smiled instantly.

"They are not." She threw another punch.

Reece laughed and pulled the mitt off. He shook his hand.

"Okay, good enough. I guess I was mistaken." He stepped closer, less than a breath away, as his eyes moved to hers. "Your eyes are perfect," he whispered, and she felt her knees go weak.

Her eyes darted down to his lips as she remembered how they had felt next to her own. How he had tasted when his tongue had dipped into her mouth and played with hers.

"Hailey?" Reece said softly.

"Yes?" she asked, jerking her eyes upward again.

"I really want to kiss you again," he said, but then he surprised her by taking a huge step backwards. "How about I show you a few moves to help you get away from a mugger?"

She swallowed the lump in her throat and nodded in agreement, needing more space between them.

But what happened over the next few minutes could not be considered hands off. Reece came up behind her and grabbed her over and over again like a mugger would, and she could barely concentrate on the moves she was supposed to do to shake free of his hold.

"I think we're done working on this move for now," Reece finally said when she was winded and tired. "We can practice it again next time. How about some boxing?" He rolled his shoulders. When she nodded, he asked, "How's the bathroom coming along?"

"Wonderfully. I promised Harper I'd help tomorrow, since I have the day off." She took a sip from her water bottle as he slipped the gloves out of his bag.

"If you need any help, I'm always available," he offered, holding the gloves out for her to slip them on.

"Thanks, but honestly, the bathroom isn't all that big.

From the looks of it, they don't really need my help. I'm just..." She bit her bottom lip while Reece waited, his dark eyebrows arched. She took a deep breath. "You know Nick pretty well, right?"

He nodded. "We've been friends our entire lives."

"Do you trust him? Would you trust him with your sister?"

Reece smiled. "I'm pretty sure my sister is a goner for Wyatt, seeing as they're engaged and all..."

She rolled her eyes and broke in. "You know what I mean." She threw the first punch at the weighted bag while he held it for her.

Reece's smile slipped. "I would trust Nick with my life and the lives of my entire family. He's a good guy. Through and through," he said soberly. "Whatever is between him and Harper, trust me, Nick is one man in Pride you shouldn't worry about."

Hailey took a deep breath and nodded. "Thanks, I figured as much."

Chapter Four

Reece knew there was something eating at Hailey. Her eyes were still a little puffy, and it was obvious she was upset.

"Is that why you were crying earlier?" he asked. He saw her tension return. When she didn't respond, he placed his hands lightly on her shoulders. "If you trust my opinion of Nick, you should trust me enough to tell me what's bothering you."

She shrugged and then hit the bag a few more times as he held it.

"Tell me about you." She punched the bag. "We've been talking a lot about me."

"Okay, what do you want to know?" he asked while she continued to throw punches.

"Have you lived in Pride your entire life?"

"Yes," he answered easily.

"No college?" She threw a punch after every question.

"No. Move your shoulder down," he corrected.

She did as he suggested and threw a couple more punches.

"Good." He nodded for her to continue asking questions.

"Girlfriends? Ever married?" she asked between blows.

"Nope. Last girlfriend I had was about two years ago. I'm focused on my career."

"Boxing?" she asked and he nodded. "Are you any good at it?"

He chuckled. "Current reigning champ in my weight class."

She stopped, her hands up like he'd taught her. "Wow, really?"

He nodded again. "I have the trophy and belt to prove it. Want to see?" He smiled.

"Belt?" She shook her head. "I don't really follow boxing."

His smile slipped a little. "You get a belt. I'll show you a picture." He grabbed his phone, and pulled it out.

"Is this your dog?" she asked.

He smiled. "Yeah, that's Ali." He smiled as she looked at the photo of the little yellow lab puppy that he'd gotten a few weeks earlier.

"That's Lucy's brother?" She smiled at the photo of the dog holding a huge stick on the beach during their last walk.

"Yup."

"Where is he now?" she asked, handing him back his phone.

"Home. I've kennel trained him. We take long runs on the beach first thing in the morning and when I get home at night. He's got a lot of energy."

"Lucy and Harper take long walks in the woods." She took his phone when he found the image of him holding up his belt.

"Wow," she said, her eyes scanning the photo. "You're

bleeding." She glanced up at him, her eyes going to the small scar he'd gained that day just above his right eye.

"It happens sometimes." He shrugged.

"Why boxing?" She handed him back his phone.

"I suppose it calms me down and thrills me at the same time," he admitted.

She was quiet for a moment. "I don't think I could ever willingly walk into something where I knew I could be hurt."

"I don't focus on that. I focus on determining my opponents moves, their weaknesses, and their strategies." He thought about it. "And winning." He smiled.

She was smiling when he tucked his phone back into his bag.

"What do your folks think?" she asked as he moved back behind the bag and threw a few more punches.

"They are proud. My mother used to be squeamish, but after I won a few fights and she understood I wasn't going to stop, she got behind me all the way. She even comes down here and works out with me a few times each month."

"Your mother boxes?" Hailey asked, dropping her arms.

"Yup, and my dad and I get in the ring." He nodded towards the boxing ring across the room from them. "He used to kick my butt when I was younger. Now I have to make sure I don't hurt him." He laughed, then realized she was frowning down at her gloved hands. "What about your parents?"

She shrugged. "We don't have any." She tried to remove the gloves.

He walked over and undid the Velcro. She removed the gloves and took a sip of her water.

"I'm sorry," he said, sitting beside her. "Did they die?"

"Our mother did," she said, avoiding his gaze. "We never knew our fathers."

He was quiet for a moment. "You and Harper have different fathers?"

"We think so." She leaned back against the wall.

"This stalker you and Harper have talked about. Who is he to you?" he asked, curious.

At first, when she'd talked about the trouble they were in, he'd thought it was possibly one of their ex-husbands or boyfriends. But then why would both of them afraid? That led him to think that it was a family member instead.

"Someone from our past," she finally said, closing her eyes and rolling her head back.

"Is he dangerous?" he asked, trying a different tactic. Instead of getting specifics about who it was, he would just try to find how much danger they were in.

"He is the reason we've jumped at shadows for the past six years," she said, sounding weary.

"My offer to teach your sister still stands." He wanted to reach over and take her hand in his, but he left them resting on his knees.

"Thanks, I think Nick is helping her." She glanced at him. "I think she's avoiding staying at his place because of me. She doesn't want me to be alone."

He thought of inviting her to stay at his place but then shook that thought off. After all, he'd just gotten her to trust him enough to let him kiss her. What would an invitation like that do to her? She'd probably run for the hills.

"I'm going to shower." She stood up suddenly.

"Hailey," he said, stopping her. "Whatever is chasing you, both of you, I can help. This town can help."

She nodded once and then disappeared into the locker room.

Feeling slightly frustrated, he headed to shower off.

So much had changed in the time he'd known her. He had changed his life goals. His dreams.

There had been a time he'd wanted to be top of the charts in the boxing world. Travel. Fame. Money.

Now, he spent more time at home working for his dad so he could be close to her. And in all that time, he'd only kissed her once.

He'd never waited so long for so little promise before. Not that his only reason for sticking around Hailey was the possibility of sex. But it was one reason.

He'd grown up with parents who, after almost thirty years of marriage, still loved each other, and he knew that he didn't want a relationship that was based solely on sex. Taking a full year to get to know Hailey, ease her into feeling comfortable about having a friendship first, had been important to him.

Now, it seemed, so was making sure she was comfortable physically around him.

He needed her to understand that, whatever happened between them, he wasn't going to overpower her.

Honestly, he liked knowing that she could take care of herself, to stand up against any threat.

It was one of the things he found sexy in a woman, her ability to fight against any aggressor.

Maybe it was all the years of being bullied or because the main person who had bullied him had been a girl. Either way, every time she hit the punching bag, his feelings for her grew.

Whenever he saw her stand up for herself, his desire for her doubled.

When she talked about her past, he could see the pain and hurt. That had his emotions for her twisting as well. He wanted to protect her. It was as innate as his desire to protect his own family. He had spoken the truth. Hailey and her sister were protected by everyone in the small town.

They were a part of Pride now.

Just as he stepped out of the shower, his cell phone rang.

It was his manager, Aaron, and he answered the call as he wrapped a towel around his hips.

"Hey, Aaron."

"Reece, buddy," Aaron Hunt practically shouted.

The man was one of the best boxing managers on the West Coast. He'd been in the industry for over twenty years and had managed some of the best names to hold a title. The man was a household name to anyone who followed boxing.

The only problem with Aaron was that he always shouted. As if he'd spent one too many hours in a crowded arena and had lost control of his volume button.

"What's up, Aaron?" Reece asked, reminding himself not to raise his own volume to match Aaron's.

"Vegas, are you ready for your match?" Aaron asked.

"Sure am," he answered with a smile. "I've been hitting the gym every day." He sat on the bench and held his phone slightly away from his ear.

"Good, good. I've got everything arranged. You have a suite at the Aria. Your airline tickets are all set too. You should see all the details in your email."

"Great." He smiled as he thought about competing again.

It had been a little over a month since he'd stepped into the ring for an actual fight.

People weren't all that interested in watching boxing during the holidays.

"Let me know if you need anything," Aaron added.

"Will do."

"See you there," Aaron said, and then hung up.

That was another thing about Aaron. He was short and to the point, as if he had a million other things to do.

He got dressed and stepped out of the locker room. He decided to wait for Hailey to finish cleaning up. He knew she'd been enjoying the showers there, so it wasn't surprising that he'd beat her out of the locker room.

He sat on a bench and sent his family a text message with his fight details.

His sister instantly replied with an invitation to dinner.

"Heard you and Hailey have been hanging. You should bring her to dinner next weekend before you head to Vegas."

"Is Wyatt cooking?" he joked.

"No, I was going to make your favorite," Hannah responded.

Reece frowned, remembering the last time his sister had cooked for him.

He loved Hannah. Really. Still, the last thing he wanted to do was to force Hailey to eat one of Hannah's home-cooked meals.

It wasn't that she was a terrible cook. Well, yes, she was a terrible cook.

Then Hailey stepped out of the dressing room, and he desperately wanted a dozen excuses to spend time with her. Even if that meant dinner with his sister.

Chapter Five

When Hailey came out of the locker room, Reece was sitting on the bench waiting for her. He'd obviously showered and was looking down at his phone with a frown on his lips.

She'd thought of telling him everything earlier, opening up to him about her and Harper's past. The things that they had gone through in their childhood. The things they were running from. The person they were hiding from. But she'd chickened out and had disappeared as quickly as she could into the locker room.

"Problems?" she asked him. She sat next to him to retie her shoe, which had come loose.

"No, just... My sister wants to cook me dinner." He rolled his eyes.

"What's wrong with that?"

"She wants me to invite you along too."

Hailey smiled. "I like your sister."

"She's not a very good cook. I mean, she's okay, but..." He shrugged. "I'm much better."

"Oh?" She couldn't help but laugh. "I'm far worse than Harper. She can make a fish on an open flame taste like pure heaven." She sighed, remembering all the times that her sister had turned stale crackers and a fish that they had caught in the stream behind their home into a wonderful meal.

"Maybe for our second date, I can cook for you?" he offered.

She stiffened. She'd thought of a million excuses to get out of going on a date with him. Fear crept into her mind whenever she thought of going out with him.

She didn't know how to act on a date. In all of the movies and shows she'd watched, dates were, well, awkward. Hailey avoided awkward situations as much as she could.

"I'd better get going," she said, suddenly.

"Are we still on to practice those self-defense moves tomorrow? I have some time around two."

She wanted to turn him down, but then she remembered how bad she was at breaking out of his hold. What if she was put in that position again? Could she get out of it? She didn't want Harper to feel responsible like last time. She knew that her sister would carry the guilt for what had happened to her for the rest of her life, even though Harper couldn't have done anything to protect Hailey. Hell, she couldn't even protect herself back then.

"Sure," she said. She stepped outside and took a deep breath of cold crisp Oregon air.

This was so much better than where she'd grown up. It had always been muggy. Hot. Sticky.

She felt a shiver race down her spine and glanced around the dark parking lot. Just then, Reece stepped out behind her.

"Are you okay?" He stopped beside her and turned to look at where she'd just been looking.

She shook off the feeling of being watched and nodded. "Just enjoying the fresh air." She started towards her truck.

"Drive safe, the roads are a little slick," Reece called after her.

"Thanks, you too." She got in her truck. As she pulled out of the parking lot, she glanced back at the bushes and felt another shiver race down her spine.

She hated the feeling of being watched. It had been years since she'd felt the need to jump at shadows. But knowing that her sister was worried about their past coming after them had put her on edge.

When she pulled into the driveway, she could tell that Harper was still awake.

She stepped into the house and smiled when she smelled cookies and popcorn.

Her sister was sitting on the sofa watching a movie and hit pause when she came in.

After giving Lucy a little attention, Hailey sat next to Harper.

"So, how was it?" Harper asked.

She shrugged. "I pretty much kicked Reece's butt."

Harper smiled. "That's my girl."

Hailey laughed. "I smell cookies."

Harper jumped up and rushed to the kitchen and came back with a bowl of cookies and caramel popcorn.

"I can restart the movie if you want." She motioned to the television.

"No, I've seen it. Just hit play. We'll watch it from here." She tucked her feet under herself and snuggled up with her sister to watch the action flick while Lucy snuggled up next to Harper.

The next morning, Nick arrived with breakfast sandwiches and fresh coffee for the three of them.

After eating, they headed into the bathroom, where Nick started putting up the tiles. He would need to cut some of them on a saw he'd brought with him.

She watched the progress with interest and even stepped in a few times to learn how to place the tiles between the small spacers.

Nick was patient with them and talked them through the process.

By lunchtime, she was sweaty and in need of another shower. She was thankful she'd agreed to meet with Reece, since it gave her an excuse to shower at the Boys and Girls Club again.

After Nick placed the last tile, they all stood back and admired how wonderful it looked.

"It will have to dry overnight. Tomorrow we can grout," he told them. "If you need, you both are welcome to use the guest shower at my place."

"Are we that ripe?" Hailey joked. She'd pretty much made up her mind about Nick. As Reece said, he was a very nice guy. She trusted Reece's opinion of him and trusted Harper's choice to trust Nick.

"No, just offering," Nick said, sounding a little embarrassed.

"Thanks, but I've been using the showers at the club." She glanced down at her watch. "I have another session with Reece in an hour. I'll get my things and head down early so I don't knock him out with my stench." She laughed as she left the kitchen.

She put a fresh pair of workout clothes and street clothes in her backpack, then headed out.

Since she was early, she took her time showering off before dressing in her workout clothes.

When she stepped out into the gym, Reece was there punching the weighted bag.

She'd never seen him working out before and doubted he even knew she was there watching him.

He was wearing gym shorts—the kind the basketball players wore—tennis shoes, and a white tank top. He had the small gloves on and was hitting the bag so hard it swayed with each blow.

His arms were filled with lean muscles, the kind that would normally scare her. But she couldn't take her eyes from them now. Her legs actually felt weak as she watched him.

When he caught sight of her, his entire demeanor changed. He'd been focused on his stance, the way he hit the bag before. Now his shoulders dropped, and his hands lay by his sides. His look of concentration was gone, replaced by a grin that had her body reacting in a way it never had before.

"Oh, hey, I didn't know you were here." He removed his gloves as he walked towards her.

Without thinking, she stepped up to him, lifted onto her toes, and kissed him.

"Wow," he said when she jerked back, shocked at the move she'd just made.

"Sorry." She blushed, embarrassed that she'd done it wrong.

She turned to rush away but stopped when he gently laid a hand on her arm.

"Hailey, don't be embarrassed and don't rush away," he said softly. "I enjoy kissing you and, even more, I enjoy you kissing me." He smiled. She nodded once, avoiding his eyes. "Come on, let's see if you can kick my butt and get away from a mugger." He wiggled his eyebrows.

She moved over to the mats and got into position.

"I've got a match in Vegas in a couple weeks," Reece said, following her.

"A match?" She frowned.

"Boxing. I'm fighting Robert Carrigan Jr," he said. She waited, unsure of what to say. "He's the current champion in the next class." He added. "If I beat him, I'll step up a class. It's a big deal."

"How wonderful. Do you get hurt fighting?" she asked, worried.

He smiled and shook his head. "Not usually. I mean, I could. I've broken my nose twice." He shrugged as if it wasn't a big deal. She cringed, remembering the one time she'd broken her nose. Her mother had thrown a beer bottle at her head, and she hadn't been fast enough to duck.

"I broke my nose once. It's not fun." She tied her hair up and got into position.

"Have you ever been to Vegas?" he asked as he reached for her and she dodged him.

"Yes, we stayed there for a short time." She tried to focus on dodging his attacks.

"You should come with me," he said, getting his hands on her upper arms.

She swung out and almost escaped his hold, only to be turned around and fully engulfed in his arms.

"Do you know where you messed up?" he asked, his mouth right next to her ear. She felt a shiver of heat race through her entire body as she shook her head from side to side.

"You dodged instead of ducked." He released her and

they went through the motions again, only this time he stopped right before he spun her around. "Here, tuck your chin in to your chest, and roll." He took his free hand, placed it on top of her head, and nudged her downward. "Go to your knees and roll," he said, and she followed along, completely escaping his hold. "Good, now try it again."

By the third try, she was fully escaping his hold without him pulling back.

"Good. Now that you have that down, how about we try from behind?" He turned her away from him.

It took more than a dozen tries for her to halfway escape his hold from behind. The entire time, she tried to not focus on how wonderful it was to have Reece's arms around her.

"Let's move on," Reece said after her last attempt ended with her on the ground and him hovering above her, smiling down at her.

"This wouldn't be so hard if you weren't so big," she pointed out as he helped her up from the mat.

"My sister learned how to escape me, and she's shorter than you are. It's all about training," he said. "You'll get it. Eventually."

She shook her head. "I'm not a big fighter."

He was silent for a moment. "No one wants to be. But circumstances can force us to stand up for ourselves and the ones we love."

The sincerity in his tone made her eyes burn as memories flooded her mind. Before she knew what she was doing, she rushed from the room. She only stopped when the cold air hit her. Gulping it in, she counted her heartbeats until her body was back under control.

"Are you okay?" Reece asked from directly behind her.

He'd been standing inches away from her, waiting until

she had herself back under control. She'd felt his presence, but he'd held off from touching her.

She nodded her head without looking at him and took one last deep breath.

"Harper thinks it's her responsibility to protect me." She wrapped her arms around herself. Now that she was calm, the chill in the air washed through her.

"Big sisters are like that," he said. "Hannah still thinks she has to watch out for me."

Hailey glanced at him and almost laughed. "You're much bigger than she is."

He shrugged. "Not in her mind. To her, I'm still the skinny kid that followed her around and skinned my knees when she wasn't there to catch me."

She smiled for a moment, then turned to him. "I need to prove to her that I can protect myself. That she doesn't have to put her life on hold any longer because of me."

He was quiet for a moment, then said, "From what I've seen, she hasn't put her life on hold. It seems that she and Nick are getting pretty serious."

She turned around. "If he asked her to move in with him, she'd say no."

Reece nodded. "I can see that. She wants to make sure you're safe. With this stalker the two of you are worried about..." He dropped off. "I wish Harper would let me teach her too."

"She says that she's learning from Nick and that he's teaching her to shoot too." She sighed. "I didn't even know that she liked guns."

"Don't you?" he asked.

She shook her head. "No, they scare me just as much as..." She closed her eyes. "No."

"How about we grab some dinner at the Golden Oar?" he suggested. "I think we've had enough for today."

She thought about going home to an empty house. Harper had texted her that she was going to Nick's to use his shower.

"Sure," she agreed eagerly.

Chapter Six

Walking into the restaurant beside Hailey gave him warm fuzzy feelings. It felt good. Right. A-freaking-mazing.

He knew he was pushing her limits when he reached over and took her hand. He felt her slightly jerk her hand, but seconds later her fingers relaxed in his.

They were seated at a table by the fireplace. They ordered sodas and quietly looked over the menus.

"This is..." she started but then stopped and shook her head, disappearing behind the menu.

"What?" he asked.

"Nothing." She continued to hide her face.

"Hailey." He nudged the menu down. "Talk to me." He could tell that she was embarrassed by whatever she was about to say. "Whatever it is, I promise I won't laugh."

She set her menu down and took a deep breath. "A lot of people come here for dates, right?"

He frowned as he nodded. "I suppose they do. But I had somewhere else in mind for our first date." He leaned on the table slightly. "When is your next day off?"

She tilted her head slightly as she thought. He couldn't help but smile at her look of concentration.

"A little over a week, I think. I'll have to check the schedule," she finally answered. "I'm actually going to be working a few double shifts."

He nodded and leaned back. "When you know for sure, let me know. I'll arrange everything."

She smiled and then went back to looking at the menu. "I don't know why I'm looking at this." She set it aside. "I always get the same thing."

"Me too." He chuckled. "Burger?"

She nodded. "Why are they so good here?"

"The truffle fries are amazing too." He felt his stomach growl.

"Aren't boxers supposed to be on some sort of strict diet?" she asked, taking a sip of her drink.

"Some are, not me." He shrugged. "Since I work out regularly, my metabolism is pretty regulated."

"I have to limit my pizza and pasta intake," she said with a chuckle. "I suppose I need to work out more often."

"We've been hitting it pretty hard the last couple nights. I'd say you've earned the burger and fries."

"Even if I haven't, I'm still getting them." She laughed, and he couldn't stop himself from matching her smile.

Her smile and laughter were addictive.

The more they chatted, the more he lost himself in her. He kept his questions away from her past even as she dug further into his. He didn't mind. He had nothing to hide.

His life growing up in the small town was no secret. Everyone who lived in Pride knew everything about him and his family.

Hell, he doubted he could sneeze without someone knowing about it.

Even just sitting at the restaurant with Hailey, he knew that word was spreading about them being together. Not that he minded. Everyone he knew had asked him when he was going to ask her out.

He couldn't even have a crush on someone without the townspeople knowing.

If it bothered him, he would have moved out of town long ago. In a way, everyone around him helped to hold him accountable.

When he needed help, there was always someone a phone call away.

By the time they walked out of the restaurant, he had convinced himself that Hailey was far better than he deserved.

She was smart, witty, kind, and made him laugh like no other person ever had.

"Thanks for tonight," Hailey said as she leaned against her truck.

He moved slightly closer to her.

"All I did was enjoy your company," he admitted truthfully.

"You make me feel fluttery when you stand so close," she said softly.

He couldn't help it, his smile grew when he heard that.

She pointed at him. "That makes it even worse."

"What?" he asked with a chuckle.

"Your smile."

He moved a little closer.

"How does it make you feel when I do this?" he laid his hand gently on her hip and heard her suck in a deep breath.

"Hot," she whispered.

"And this?" He leaned in, just a breath from her lips.

Instead of answering, her eyes darted down to his lips, inviting him.

When he tasted her, a soft groan escaped her lips.

"You're the sweetest thing I've ever tasted," he admitted, dipping his tongue in for another sample.

When he lifted his hand to cup her face, she tensed and jerked back, almost as if he'd slapped her instead of gently caressing her.

He took a giant step back.

"Sorry," she said, avoiding his gaze. "I... I'd better go."

He stopped her by taking her hand in his.

"I don't ever want to make you afraid." He lifted her chin until their eyes met. "Talk to me. Tell me where your lines are that I shouldn't cross."

She swallowed slowly, then nodded. "Goodnight."

"Night." He stood back to let her go. He watched her taillights disappear before getting into his truck and driving home.

Ali was waiting for him to let him out. As he stood on his deck, watching his dog sniff every bush in his yard, he wondered what it would take for Hailey to open up to him.

Almost half an hour after getting home, his phone rang. Seeing Tom's number, he answered.

"Hey, what's up?" he asked, knowing his friend never called him this late unless something was wrong.

"You might want to head on over here to Harper and Hailey's cabin. Someone broke in—"

"What?" he interrupted. "Are they okay?"

"They're fine. Nick is here now. We're checking the place out again, but I figured you'd want to know."

"Thanks, I'm heading there now," he said, grabbing his keys.

The cabin was typically ten minutes away from his place. He made it there in under eight.

Seeing the police car and Tom's Jeep in the driveway, he parked and jumped out of his truck.

"Hailey?" Reece called out,

"Here." Hailey rushed into his arms, and he held onto her for a moment.

Then Hailey awkwardly pulled away from him, as if she was embarrassed to hug him in front of her sister.

"Are you okay?" Reece asked, looking towards the cabin. When he spotted Tom and Nick, he nodded a greeting in their direction.

"Yes, the place was empty when I got home," Hailey said, wrapping her arms around herself. She looked tired and scared, and he wanted to hold onto her a little more, but he knew she wasn't comfortable being so close to him at the moment.

Instead, he walked over and shook Nick's and Tom's hands. "Anything disturbed?" he asked, his eyes still on the cabin.

"Just the shower we worked hard to rebuild today," Hailey groaned beside him. "Looks like we'll need to buy more tile." She rolled her eyes.

"Grab your things," Harper told Hailey. "Nick has offered to put us up at his place. Until we know who did this, we're staying there."

"No, I can't." Hailey shook her head. "I won't run and hide. Besides, I refuse to be a third wheel in whatever this is." She motioned towards her sister and Nick.

"You could stay at my place," Reece jumped in, not sure why. He only knew that he wanted to keep her safe.

Hailey's eyebrows shot up as she looked at him. "Thanks, but no. I'm staying put."

"If she stays, so do I," Harper said.

"Then I'll camp out here," Reece said quickly. There was no way he was going to leave the sisters alone and afraid. He could see it in both of their eyes.

"Ditto," Nick added.

Both of the sisters sighed and then looked at one another.

"It may only be for a few nights," Tom jumped in. "You're welcome to come stay with Kate and I, but you'd have to sleep in a single bed," he added.

After an awkward moment of silence, Hailey threw up her hands. "Fine." She turned to him. "I'll stay with you. I am not going to spend a night listening to them. Seeing them kiss once was enough for me." She rolled her eyes but there was a smile on her lips.

Reece couldn't help but smile at Hailey's humor at a time of unease.

"I'll help you get your things," he said and then followed Hailey inside the cabin.

He had never been in the cabin before. The place was in better condition than he'd thought it would be, knowing it had sat abandoned for years until the sisters had moved in.

He looked around briefly as he followed Hailey back to a bedroom.

She tossed a large black bag on her bed. To his surprise, the thing was already full of clothes.

"It's my bug-out bag," she said with a sigh. "Harper makes me keep it ready just in case."

He wanted to ask her why, but he just stood there as she dumped more clothes into the massive thing. Then she disappeared and came back with a smaller bag and tossed it in as well. He assumed it was her toiletry items from the bathroom he'd seen at the end of the hallway. He'd seen the destruction even from here. The room looked like it had exploded. Pieces of tile were everywhere.

Her room was painted a dark sky blue. The room was pretty empty except for a mattress that sat on an old bed frame. An old end table that she was using as a nightstand sat next to it.

There were banners or posters on the wall of pretty scenery and a horse running in a field.

"Do you like horses?" he asked, motioning towards the poster.

She shrugged. "I've never been near one, so I don't really know. I like looking at them though." She pulled a coat from her closet and put it on. "I think I've got everything." She turned towards him. "I'm only staying with you because I know my sister won't let this go. She believes I'm safe with you."

"You are," he assured her.

He carried her bag out to his truck, but she wanted her own truck with her, so she followed him to his place.

When they parked, he could hear Ali barking, and he realized he'd left in such a hurry, he'd forgotten to put the dog in his kennel.

"Sorry," he said as he pulled her suitcase out of the truck. "I forgot to put Ali up. Hopefully, he hasn't messed up the house."

Hailey smiled. "Lucy learned early not to mess with anything if she wanted to be left out again." She stopped at the base of his front steps and looked up at his home. "Wow, it's bigger than I thought it would be."

He nodded. "It doesn't look big from the road. Come on in. Make yourself at home while you're here." He stopped suddenly. "I mean that sincerely."

She smiled and nodded. "Thanks."

"I'll give you a quick tour after we put your things in the guest room." He glanced around the house as Ali jumped up to eagerly greet Hailey.

"He looks so much like Lucy and Blue." She laughed and then nudged Ali down.

Reece snapped his fingers. It didn't appear the dog had messed with anything, so he gave him praise for a moment.

"I really appreciate you allowing me to stay here," she said as she removed her coat.

"I'm just thankful Nick and I don't have to camp out in your driveway."

Her eyes narrowed, but then she nodded. "I prefer not to run..."

"From the man who is stalking you and your sister?" he asked. He wanted to give her space, but at the same time he needed to know just what he was up against. What he was protecting her from.

She nodded slowly. "His name is..." She paused for just a heartbeat. "Fred."

"And he is..." He waited.

She shrugged. "He was our mother's boyfriend."

His entire body relaxed. Not her boyfriend. Not her ex.

Then her eyes moved up to his. "The man who beat and raped Harper and me when we were kids."

Chapter Seven

She knew it was a lot to take in. The look on Reece's face said it all. She was relieved to have told him. She'd wanted to tell someone, to get it off her chest, and he was the person that she was the closest to, the person she wanted to get closer with. She'd decided to tell him a few days before after having a long talk with her sister.

She decided to leave a more detailed conversation until later.

"Show me around." She motioned. "We can talk later."

He nodded, then picked up her bag.

His house was shaped like a big U. They had parked at a detached garage, then had walked up three cement stairs to a patio area where two large glass doors sat.

In the entryway there was a table with bright yellow flowers sitting on it and a painting of a yellow sunflower hanging on the wall above it.

She followed Reece to the left and stepped into a massive living room space. Soft cream sofas and chairs sat across from a stone fireplace that had white and cream bookcases on either side of it.

There was a half wall separating the front door from the living room area. The space looked cozier than anything she'd ever seen before.

"Wow," she said softly.

"The bedrooms are upstairs. There is a guest room downstairs, but I think you'll be warmer and more comfortable upstairs." He motioned to a set of wood stairs that sat between the living room and the entryway. "We'll head up there first, then I'll show you around," he suggested. She nodded, then followed him up the L-shaped stairs.

There were two hallways, one leading to the right, which he took, and another across from a large open space that looked down to the living room below.

"My bedroom is across there on the left." He motioned as he opened a door. "This is your room." He stepped in and set her bag down just inside the door. "The bathroom is through there." He motioned to a doorway. "Closet." He motioned to another door. "There's a balcony. On a clear day you can see Pride Harbor."

The queen-sized bed had a fancy black iron headboard and a white quilt that was so pretty she was afraid to touch it. Pillows in a variety of shades of blue sat on the bed along with a dark blue throw blanket.

The nightstands were cream colored, matching the walls. A blue and cream rug sat under the bed.

"This is amazing." She walked over to look into the bathroom and gasped.

White tiles went up each wall to just below her shoulders. The rest of the walls were painted a soft yellow. The bathroom had an older style but somehow looked brand new. There were mirrors above the classic dual sinks.

It was nicer than any bathroom she'd ever seen.

The shower was done in the same white tiles, but there

was a vertical line of ocean-blue tiles streaking down to the floor. A wall of glass separated the shower from the rest of the bathroom.

There was a three-quarter wall separating the toilet from the shower area.

"You told me you were still working on fixing this place up." She narrowed her eyes at him.

He chuckled. "Yes, it's why I didn't put you in the bedroom downstairs. Plus, there's..." He shook his head. "I'll show you." He motioned and she followed him out of the room.

They walked down the hallway and took the hallway to his room.

When she stepped into his room, she was again shocked at the beauty of the space.

There was a fireplace opposite his bed with small bookcases on each side. The walls were a sky blue with white paneling on the lower half. An entire wall of windows sat opposite the doorway.

"I get the same view here as your room." He motioned to the windows in the bedroom. "Then there is this space in here." He opened the door to his closet. A small rack of clothes hung in the middle of the room and there was an old dresser.

"I have no idea what to do in here. The space is massive. Bigger than anything I would ever need." He sighed as she walked in. It was almost two stories high and bigger than the living room at the cabin.

The walls were a dark brown color and had been patched up in several places.

"For now, it's the last thing on my list." He leaned against the doorway. "There are several rooms like this one that I have yet to get to."

She nodded. "What about your bathroom?"

He smiled. "It was one of the first rooms that I did." He motioned and she followed him to his bathroom.

It was a lot like the bathroom that was attached to the guest room, only double the size. It had a tall wall separating the toilet from everything else in place of the three-quarter wall in the other bathroom.

This shower was easily twice as big. It had a glass wall and was attached to a massive jet tub. There was even a fireplace at the end of the tub.

She'd never seen anything like it.

"Do you ever use that?" she asked, motioning to the tub.

He chuckled and nodded. "I pour ice into it after a fight that didn't go so well and do ice baths. Other than that, no. I've never soaked in it. I have a hot tub out on the deck that I use instead."

She nodded, feeling suddenly stupid, so she bent down and scratched Ali's head.

"The other bedroom on this floor is next to your room. I haven't touched it yet. Your bathroom joins with it. You can check it out later if you want. For now, let's head downstairs so I can show you the rest of the place."

She followed him back down the stairs. At the base of the stairs, he turned left and went back down the hallway by the front door.

"This is the mud room, laundry room, and pantry all in one. It leads back to the kitchen." He opened a door, and she looked into a large laundry slash mud room. There was a long bench where someone could sit to remove their shoes, and there were little cubbies to store them in. There were hooks for keys, coats, or hats, and bins above for gloves or scarfs.

He had two coats and a couple of hats hanging on the

hooks, and a pair of hiking boots and mud boots in the cubbies.

Everything was tidy. Neat. Clean.

Much like she and Harper kept their home.

The laundry area was just as organized and clean.

Then Reece opened the door to the pantry. It was huge. Wood shelves lined the two walls on either side of the narrow room. There was a door at the other end, and she followed Reece through it into the kitchen.

She took note of a small bar area in the pantry that he had set up with a coffee station.

"Help yourself to anything in here," he said before stepping out into the kitchen.

The kitchen was not what she expected. It was all white. Everywhere.

"I haven't fully remodeled this room yet," Reece said with a slight frown. "It needs color."

"Yes," she agreed.

The white cabinets and countertops gave it a very sterile feeling. The space was huge and the appliances were nice, but the rest of the space was just... plain.

The small dining room attached to the space was warm and cozy, and had large windows that looked outside. Even though it was dark out, she could just tell that the view would be amazing.

He had a large circular oak table with modern-looking wicker and leather chairs. A built-in hutch filled the side wall that separated that space from the living room.

The hardwood floors were covered with a thick cream, gray, and blue rug.

They took the two steps down into that space.

"Formal dining room is back there." He motioned to the room behind the stairs just off to the other side of the kitchen. "I haven't decorated or used that space yet." He shrugged. "Actually, I've got some storage boxes still in there." He rolled his eyes. "We can head downstairs."

She followed him back to the main staircase, and they went down this time.

They stepped directly into a large room with wood paneling on all the walls. Here, she could see the outdated feel of the home.

The floors needed a shine. The dark paneling was a lot like the stuff in the cabin that she and Harper had cleaned when they'd first moved in.

There were built-in bookshelves and cabinets along a long wall that separated the larger space from a hallway, which she guessed led to the bedroom area.

He had an old sofa, a coffee table, and a ping-pong table set up in the space.

After he flipped on the outside lights, she could see that there was a wall of glass that led out to a massive patio area complete with a firepit, grill, patio furniture, and the hot tub.

"I can show you around outside tomorrow in the daylight." He flipped off the lights and turned to head down two more stairs. "This is my favorite room." He smiled and opened the door.

She stepped into a massive home gym. There were several boxing bags, including two weighted ones that hung from the ceiling.

Several rows of weights sat in front of an entire wall of mirrors. He also had an exercise bike and a treadmill.

The floor was covered with black and red cushions that fit the space perfectly.

"Why do you use the Boys and Girls Club if you have your own gym?" she asked.

"I supposed I'm accustomed to going there. I grew up not having a private gym. Plus, I like to get out of the house once and a while." He smiled and shrugged. "There's a bathroom attached to the gym there." He pointed. "The other guest room and attached bathroom are down the hallway."

She followed him into an empty bedroom with dark walls and a bathroom that hadn't been remodeled. "That's pretty much it."

She wanted to remind him that her entire cabin could fit on one floor of his place, but she bit her bottom lip instead.

"How about we head back upstairs? I'd like a cup of coffee."

She nodded and followed him back upstairs. She noticed that he flipped off all the lights as they went.

Ali followed them and when they stepped into the kitchen, the dog plopped down on his dog bed by the sliding door that led out to the deck area.

"Isn't he lonely?" she asked, sitting at the bar area while he moved into the pantry to make them each a cup of coffee.

"Who? Ali?" He chuckled. "No. My parents' dogs come over a lot. Plus, I'm pretty sure he and Blue and Lucy will be seeing plenty of each other. Plus, my sister and Wyatt have taken one of the puppies from that litter too. A girl named Luna." He smiled as he set a mug in front of her. "Cream? Sugar?"

"Black."

He shook his head as he walked over to the fridge and poured some cream into his coffee. "Never understood anyone who drank it black."

"Thank you." She looked down into the dark mug.

How many nights had she gone to sleep afraid? Not just for herself but for Harper.

Those first few years on their own, Harper had worked nights, leaving Hailey alone every night. When she was a teenager, she'd fall asleep with the television on to cartoons, something she'd never had as a kid. It helped to ease her mind some, but the nightmares always came. And since Harper was never there, she'd had no one to comfort her.

Her mother certainly had never been there for either of them.

As the years went by, she'd learned to cope in other ways. Learning had always helped her. Learning, reading, and dreaming.

She read anything that she could get her hands on at first. She had never really gone to the library when she'd been a kid. She and Harper hadn't spent any more time at school than was necessary to keep child protective services off their backs.

Then one day while Harper was at work, she'd taken a walk and ended up finding a small library just down the street from the one-bedroom motel where they were staying.

The librarian was nice to her and explained how to check out books. Hailey had gotten a card and checked out a single book that first week and read it three times.

It was a book about books. She couldn't remember what she'd learned from it, but she had devoured it from cover to cover. The next time she'd gone to the library, she'd checked out half a dozen books instead.

She'd decided to take the GED when the librarian asked her why she wasn't in school and suggested it.

She'd passed her GED with flying colors, only missing two questions.

The librarian had suggested she sign up for college

classes, but then Harper had gotten spooked and they'd moved.

There hadn't been a library within miles of the next place they'd stayed.

She still thought about college classes but knew that her work schedule and the amount of money they were putting into the cabin wouldn't allow for it. What she really wanted was to run her own business. She dreamed of someday opening her very own hair salon.

"You don't have to thank me," Reece said, breaking into her thoughts. He had moved to stand across the countertop from her. His eyes moved slowly over her face. "You're spooked."

She nodded and took a deep breath. "More for Harper than myself."

Reece's eyes narrowed. She could tell he wanted to ask her about Fred. About what she'd admitted earlier.

Could she trust him with the fact that her sister had murdered their mother?

Chapter Eight

How do you go about asking someone to give you more details about being beaten and raped as a child? He knew whatever his next move was, he had to tread lightly. After all, it had taken him a full year to get her to trust him enough for a date.

"You want to know more about Fred." She sighed after taking a sip of her coffee. Then she motioned towards the living room. "How about we head in there and sit in front of the fire?"

He nodded and followed her into the living room. She sat down on the sofa, and he started a fire in the fireplace. Before sitting down, he went back into the pantry and grabbed a bag of popcorn that was made locally by one of the girls he'd dated in high school. Cyndi now had a successful business making gourmet popcorns in a variety of flavors.

He poured the entire bag into a bowl and sat next to Hailey. Ali had snuggled up against Hailey, and she was scratching his dog's head.

"I love Cyndi's popcorn," she said after taking a bite.

"Me too. I dated her in school. For all of a month." He chuckled, wanting to lighten the mood. Maybe it would help her talk about her dark past.

"I won't tell you everything," she said, suddenly. "What I feel comfortable telling you now is that Fred was in our lives for only a year or so. In that time, however, he changed everything. Our mother..." She closed her eyes for a moment and when she opened them again, she avoided his gaze by looking into the fire. "She wasn't there for us. Then Fred was there. I don't know when the abuse started with Harper. Fred used to slap us around, like our mother did. I didn't think there was more to it until the night before..." She closed her eyes again and shook her head.

He could tell she was struggling with telling him more. He could see the pain on her face even if he couldn't see her eyes.

"That's enough," he said, taking her hand in his. "For now. I don't need to know everything."

She nodded and looked down at their joined hands. "Harper is safe with Nick?"

"Yes," he said quickly. "And you're safe here," he assured her. "You think it was Fred?"

"There isn't anyone else." She finally met his eyes.

His eyes narrowed slightly as he ran through the possibilities. "Your mother?" he asked, only to remember she'd mentioned that she was gone already.

She shook her head slightly. "No, she's dead." She took her hand away from his.

He'd guessed as much but hearing her say it in a monotone assured him that she felt nothing about her mother's death.

"Why would he be coming after the two of you?" He

asked the question he'd been playing over in his head since finding out the sisters had a stalker.

She shrugged. "He's crazy or obsessed, I suppose." Her eyes moved to his. "What makes anyone mad enough to do something terrible to someone else?"

He sighed and then leaned back as he looked into the fire. "Darkness can be in anyone. I've never had something like that touch me personally, but a few fighters I've gone up against have struggled with addiction or ended up in prison because of their abusive behavior. Some can't separate the sport from their real lives." He glanced at her. "I'm not one of those. I've never hit anyone outside of the ring."

She nodded slowly. "If I'd thought that about you, I wouldn't have agreed to stay here."

He smiled as he felt warmth rush through his entire body. He wanted to kiss her. Wanted to be with her.

But he could see the rawness of the emotions she was feeling and knew that it wasn't the right time.

"You probably want to head up and get some sleep." He started to get up, but she shook her head.

"No, it's nice just watching the fire." She shifted slightly. "I like your home."

"I'm glad you decided to stay here."

"Me too."

They watched the fire until the embers burned out while they chatted and enjoyed their popcorn and coffee. Then they headed into the kitchen and dropped their mugs in the sink. He let Ali out while Hailey headed upstairs.

He climbed into bed with Ali at his feet and fell into a deep sleep, thankful that Hailey felt safe under his roof.

The following day, he showed her around outside. She kept talking about how wonderful the view of Pride was from up there.

Even though his house was surrounded by tall trees, there were enough clearings to give him the best view around.

Shortly before lunch, Hailey headed into town for work. Less than an hour later, he showed up at Baked with his laptop and sat in a back booth to work.

"You don't have to watch over me this much," Hailey said, refilling his tea.

He chuckled. "I like working here."

She frowned at his computer screen, then shrugged as she was called to fill someone else's cup.

An hour later, Harper, Nick, and Sean, Nick's father, strolled into Baked. He nodded to the group and went back to replying to a few emails.

He was so lost in his work that he didn't see when the group left. He kept an eye on Hailey until shortly before the dinner rush. Then he headed home to let Ali out and play with the dog in the backyard.

He'd given Hailey a key to the house and, just when he was ready to head inside, she drove up and parked her truck next to his.

When Ali rushed over to greet her, she spotted him sitting on the deck by the firepit.

"How was work?" he asked when she sat next to him.

"Great, as always." She beamed at him. "It's sort of nice coming home to a dog," she said as Ali jumped up next to her and snuggled into her lap. "I thought Harper was crazy when she brought Lucy home." She glanced down at the dog, who was already snoring on her leg. "I guess in the short time since we got her, I've gotten spoiled."

He smiled. "Growing up, we always had dogs. When I moved in here, it's felt like one of the things missing to make this a real home."

She frowned down at the dog now. "We never really had a real home." She glanced up at him. "Until we moved to Pride, I didn't even know it was possible." She glanced out over the small town as the sun continued to sink over the Pacific ocean. "I won't let him take that away from us." She suddenly jerked her head towards him. "How about you give me another lesson in self-defense? I feel like kicking some butt, even if it's yours."

He laughed and stood up. "Bring it."

She stood up, dislodging the sleeping dog, and headed inside the house.

"We can use the gym downstairs," he suggested as they made their way inside. After Ali followed them into the house, he shut and locked the sliding door.

"I'll go upstairs and change." She hung her bag on a hook in the mud room.

"I'll meet you downstairs in the gym." He gave Ali a scoop of dog food before heading upstairs himself to change into his gym clothes.

When he stepped into the gym, Hailey was there, wearing a pair of those sexy tight yoga pants she always wore when they worked together. Today's color was a soft blue that matched her eyes almost perfectly.

While they were in the gym, he tried very hard to keep things professional. After all, it was his job to make sure she could protect herself or at least escape any situation.

However, whenever her body rubbed up against his, it reacted. Everything about him reacted when he was near her.

Almost an hour later, when they were both sweaty and breathing hard, he grew tired of trying to contain his desire for her.

"Enough." He walked over to the mini-fridge and

pulled out two bottles of water. After handing her one, he turned away and drank half of his water before taking a deep breath to clear his mind.

"How am I doing?" she asked after taking a sip.

"Good," he said, avoiding her gaze. He felt frustrated that he couldn't get his mind and body back under control.

"You can tell me the truth," she said, touching his arm.

He almost jerked away from her light touch. He didn't know what would happen if he really lost control around her. Whatever the possibilities, he knew he'd just end up scaring her.

"Maybe I can have Amber come over and spar with you to prove that you're almost as good as she is," he suggested as he walked over and punched the weighted bag once in frustration.

"If I'm doing so well, why are you mad at me?" Hailey asked.

He jerked his gaze towards her.

Seeing the worried look in her eyes, every ounce of frustration and desire fled his body.

"I'm not mad at you." He ran his fingers through his hair. "I'm frustrated at myself."

"For?" she asked, tilting her head slightly.

He took a deep breath and blurted out, "For wanting you so much it hurts."

He watched fear and curiosity mix in her eyes as she looked at him.

"Hailey?" he warned her as she moved forward.

She shook her head. "I... want to try..." She dropped off as she laid her hand flat on his chest, just over his heart.

When she leaned up on her toes and brushed her lips slowly, softly, across his, he almost broke.

Let her lead, he said over and over in his head.

When her tongue darted out to cross his closed lips, he closed his eyes and wished he was made of stone so he wouldn't burst into flames with desire for her.

"Since I like kissing now, maybe I'd like... more," she said against his mouth.

He almost fell over.

He gently took hold of her hips and pressed her entire body against his. He needed his desire to be pressed tight up against her soft body.

When he kissed her and pulled her further up against him, she tensed, so he dropped his hold on her and took a giant step away.

"I..." She shook her head as tears flooded her eyes. Without saying anything, she darted from the room.

Shit. He practically slammed his fist against his chest.

Shit.

For the next hour, he pummeled the heavy bag until his knuckles almost cracked and bled.

The next day, he worked at Baked again. This time, there were no emails or deadlines to keep him occupied, so he watched Hailey. Watched the people of Pride come and go.

He chatted with everyone he knew who had a moment to talk.

His sister and Wyatt came in for lunch, and he enjoyed their company for almost a full hour.

Shortly before Hailey was off work, he suggested that they head to the Golden Oar for dinner again. He knew that Harper was working that night and figured Nick would be there after he got off shift.

He was secretly hoping to get a little more detail from them on what was going on.

When they walked into the restaurant, Harper waved at them. He followed Hailey into the bar area.

"We saw your Jeep out front and thought we might join you for dinner," Hailey said. "When do you get off work?"

"Five minutes," Harper answered after looking at her watch.

"Order us a couple of burgers. We'll grab a booth," Hailey said. Harper pointed to an open booth.

"I love this place," Hailey said as she sat down. He took the seat next to her as Nick followed them and sat across from then. Moments later, Harper joined him.

"Nick has news he wants us to hear." Harper shifted to sit almost sideways in the booth.

"We found Fred," Nick said as he pulled out a printout and laid it on the table.

"What?" Hailey jerked beside him.

While Nick talked to Hailey and Harper, he read the lengthy rap sheet on the man and memorized the black and white photo.

Fredrick Leeroy, forty-eight-year-old owner of Iron Works Strip Club outside of Atlanta, Georgia. Several arrests, including drug charges and aggravated assault, were listed.

Since Reece didn't know if the image was an old one, he scanned the images of the guy's many tattoos.

Skull and bones. Knives. Naked pinup girls.

One tattoo in particular had his blood boiling.

It simply said "Virgins" with a heart over it.

He turned the page over and slid it back to Nick before Hailey could see it.

When their food arrived, the four of them were in deep conversation, speculating as to what the man wanted from the sisters.

No one mentioned the physical abuse the sisters had endured and he knew it wasn't the time or place to talk about it.

Somehow, the conversation turned to his boxing career. He was set to head out soon for a couple of big fights, one in Vegas and one after that in California. He had mentioned them to Hailey earlier and invited her to go with him to Vegas.

"Is that how you afforded your home?" Harper asked suddenly.

"Harper!" Hailey hissed, and kicked her sister under the table.

"What? I'm curious." She turned back to Reece and waited for his answer.

Suddenly, he realized that if he failed to impress Harper, his chances of being with Hailey might be in jeopardy. He'd never been as nervous answering a question as he felt at that moment.

"My boxing career is taking off, but I still work for my dad's company. I've been programming games since I was ten."

"Right," Harper said. "I'd forgotten your dad owns... Modarth?"

Reece and Nick both chuckled. "Modark," they corrected at the same time.

Harper shrugged. "We didn't play video games growing up."

"Right." Reece smiled and looked at Hailey as he mentally told himself to play the game with her soon.

After all, he'd let her in the part of his life that included boxing. If she didn't like Modark, the biggest part of his life, well, he didn't know what he'd do.

Chapter Nine

Hailey grew more comfortable each day that she stayed at Reece's place. Not only was he easy to get along with, but he was fun to be around.

He pushed her limits physically when they practiced self-defense together. He taught her how to box and showed her all of the techniques he used against his opponents.

They watched a few videos of his past fights. She thought she'd be nervous watching them, afraid of seeing him get injured.

Instead, she lost herself in the sport of it all. She even recognized a few of the moves he'd shown her and called them out each time.

A few days after Nick had filled them in on Fred's history, Harper showed up at Baked carrying a huge hot pink Classy and Sassy Bag in her arms. Her sister was practically glowing.

"What's up?" she asked, hugging her after she mentioned to Corey that she was taking her break.

"Just bought a dress," Harper said cheerfully.

"A..." Hailey had to do a double take. Without waiting

for Harper to respond, she grabbed the bag and looked inside. Sure enough, there was a pretty soft pink dress-and-sweater combo inside, along with a stylish pair of tan boots. Her sister had never worn a dress. Never. She hadn't even owned a dress until now. "Nice. What's the occasion?"

"Valentine's Day," Harper answered with a shrug. Her sister's eyes narrowed. "What's up between you and Reece?"

"I'm not sure." She frowned into her iced tea. "I mean, he's very protective. Almost brotherly," Hailey answered.

"He... he hasn't kissed you yet?" Harper asked.

Hailey shrugged, not wanting to talk about this, here, now, with her sister. It was all so... embarrassing.

Harper leaned closer and whispered, "What have you told him about... things." She glanced around.

"A lot. Not everything, but a lot."

Harper took her hand. "I hope that one day you'll feel comfortable talking with someone like I am now."

"So, Nick knows everything?" Hailey asked, her eyes searching Harper's.

"Yes," Harper answered softly.

"And... you're not in trouble?" Hailey whispered.

Harper shook her head. "No. Even after I told him everything, he didn't even look at me differently. Besides, he's the one who found out that Heidi was already dead when I..." She dropped off. Harper had filled her in on how their mother's autopsy report showed that she had died long before Harper had poisoned her drugs with rat poison. "He's gone out of his way to make me feel... different." She leaned back in the chair. "I think I'm in love."

Hailey was quiet for a moment. Her heart ached for some odd reason. Was love between a man and woman really possible? Sure, she loved Harper. That wasn't up for question. But she'd never loved anyone else. Ever.

"I don't know if I'll ever be able to trust like that," Hailey admitted, looking down as she swirled her straw in her tea. "To tell someone my biggest secret. My biggest shame." She felt her eyes sting as she remembered that night so long ago. The pain. The hurt. The shame of it all. Sure, she'd blurted out to Reece that Fred had raped both her and Harper, but the details were still hidden deep inside her. She didn't think she would ever be able to share them with anyone.

Harper reached across the table and gripped Hailey's hand so tight that Hailey looked up at her.

"Nothing you did was shameful," she asserted. "You did nothing wrong. Neither of us did."

Hailey's eyes started to tear up, but she nodded slightly.

"Are you okay staying at Reece's place? We could go home?" Harper asked.

Swallowing the emotions, she lifted her shoulders. She knew without a doubt that Harper was better off staying with Nick. She didn't want to jeopardize that. Besides, she'd just admitted that she loved the man. Hailey was not going to get in the way of her sister's happiness. Even if she couldn't have any herself.

"I know you want to be with Nick, and I also know that you wouldn't let me stay home by myself. I'm okay where I'm at for now," she said quickly.

"Why don't you come over tonight for dinner? Nick is a wonderful cook. You can see Lucy and Blue."

Sadness overtook her at the thought of losing her sister to Nick. Would they still be close even if they didn't live together again? Would her sister still love her as much or had Nick taken her place?

Hailey glanced around, needing an excuse for time to think. "I asked for a double shift. I won't get off work until late," she lied.

"Tomorrow?" Harper asked.

Hailey nodded. "If I can swing it. I'll text you." She glanced at her watch. "I'd better get back to work."

A few hours later, almost an hour after she was scheduled to be off shift, Reece walked into Baked.

"Hey," she greeted him as he approached the counter.

"Hey." He frowned at her. "I thought you were getting off a while ago?"

"I was, I..." She shrugged. "Just wanted to help out a little longer."

He nodded. "Want to order us a pie to go?"

"Sure," she said, punching in her favorite pizza. "Hawaiian okay?" she asked as she handed him a cup for a soda.

"Sure." He disappeared to grab himself a drink.

She heard her cell phone ringing in her purse under the counter and answered Nick's call.

"Where are you?" Nick asked her.

"Work," Hailey answered quickly, fear spiking in her at Nick's tone. "Why?"

"Stay put. I'm going to have Reece head your way," Nick said.

"He's already here." She glanced as Reece returned. "What's happened?" Hailey asked Nick, a little scared.

"Someone attacked Harper on the beach. She's okay, but they tried to drown her. She's warming up before the doctor gets here to look her over," Nick said quickly.

Her vision blurred for a heartbeat.

"We're heading over there," Hailey said before hanging up.

"What?" Reece asked.

"Someone tried to drown Harper." She felt her hands shake as she grabbed her purse.

"Here, I heard the whole thing," Corey said, handing Reece a pizza box. "Not sure what's inside but take it and go. Keep us posted on your sister," he told Hailey.

"Thanks," Reece said, grabbing Hailey's arm and helping her out of the building.

She was so dumbfounded that she allowed him to load her into his truck and set the warm pizza box on her lap.

Nick's place was only a couple blocks from the pizzeria.

Still, Reece's tires squealed as he came to a stop behind Nick's Jeep.

She was still in a daze as they stepped inside the home her sister was living in now.

Tom met them at the door and the words "she's upstairs" registered enough that she headed towards the staircase across the room.

Nick met her at the bottom of the stairs. "Last door on the right," he told her. "She just got out of the shower and is dressed," he said as she rushed passed him.

When she opened the door to the bedroom her sister was sharing with Nick, she almost collapsed when she saw Harper lying on the massive bed. Her skin was pale. Her long dark hair was still wet from the shower, and she was wrapped up like a mummy.

She rushed over to the bed and wrapped her arms around her.

"You're okay?" she said into Harper's hair.

"I am," Harper said softly.

It was at that moment that Hailey realized just how much her sister meant to her.

She was everything. Not only was she her sister but she

was her mother, her best friend, her world. She didn't know what she'd do if anything happened to her.

"What happened?" she asked after she leaned back.

Harper took a deep breath. "He attacked me from behind. Hit me." She touched her head, and Hailey saw the bandage. "I woke up in the water as he held me down. I thought..." Her sister's voice cracked, and Hailey pulled her close again. "He's more dangerous than before," Harper whispered. "We should run."

The thought of never seeing Reece played in her head and caused her heart to almost burst out of her chest.

"But I can't do that to Nick." Harper leaned back again. Her eyes were wet and when Hailey wiped the tears away with her fingers, Harper did the same to her. She hadn't even realized she'd been crying. "And something tells me you don't want to go."

She shook her head. "No."

Harper smiled a little. "So we stay and fight like hell."

Hailey nodded and smiled.

Just then there was a knock on the door.

"Come in," Hailey answered.

"I brought you some toast." Nick set the tray down. "Dr. Stevens is here—"

"I don't need a doctor," Harper said quickly.

"I know, but still, it would make me feel better if he took a look at that." He motioned to the side of her head. "You know, clean it up. In case I missed some dirt or sand."

Hailey took Harper's hand and nodded. "Just let him look you over. For Nick's peace of mind." She smiled, trying to offer her comfort. Besides, she was worried about her too. Her sister's eyes were a little unfocused. She'd heard that head injuries could be really bad.

"Fine." Harper motioned towards the food. "Bring that here."

When Nick set the tray down, he turned to her. "How much do you want Reece to know?" he asked Hailey.

Hailey frowned. The thought of Nick telling Reece her darkest secrets scared her even more than her telling him herself. If her sister had indeed told Nick everything... There was no way she was going to let someone else tell Reece.

It was time she ripped that bandage off herself. Completely.

"I'll tell him everything myself. For now, just... tell him that Fred attacked Harper tonight."

Nick nodded and left. Soon after, Doctor Stevens walked in. She knew the entire Stevens family and liked them all.

She sat in the corner while the man looked over her sister and cleaned the cut on Harper's head.

When they were finally alone again, she sat next to Harper once more. How many years had they been afraid of anyone outside of the two of them? Police officers, child protective services, even teachers at their school. This was probably the first time Harper had ever been examined by a doctor.

"He's nice." Hailey sighed, realizing that she should probably be seen by the doctor herself, like he'd suggested before leaving. "I suppose we need to stop fearing doctors."

Harper smiled and took her hand. "I love you."

"I love you too," Hailey said.

"I love Nick," Harper said. "I think... I think I want to move in here. To live with him. But I..." She shook her head as tears filled her eyes. "I don't want to leave you."

Hailey reached over and hugged her. "You won't be leaving me. I'll always be here."

"I won't move in here officially until after Fred is locked up," Harper said against her hair.

Hailey nodded. "I'm staying put until that man is behind bars. Reece says I can stay in his guest room for however long that takes. He's invited me to go with him to Vegas to see his fight," she admitted, suddenly feeling heated.

Harper leaned back and smiled. "You should go. We liked Vegas, remember?"

Hailey nodded as the short time that they had spent in the city replayed in her head. "Are you okay?" She brushed a strand of Harper's hair away from her face and could see happiness in her eyes.

Harper suddenly burst out crying and everything that had happened to her a few hours earlier flowed from her in almost one very long sentence. Hailey had to concentrate to understand most of her words. Harper never cried. The sound of it almost undid her.

It was obvious how scared she'd been, being held under the water. She could only imagine how terrifying it must have been. Neither of them had ever gone swimming before. They used to wade in the shallow creek to catch fish or crawdads, but they had never jumped in for fear of drowning.

She pulled Harper into her arms and settled in the bed.

"We haven't had the best past, have we?" She brushed her fingers through Harper's hair, avoiding the bandage the doctor had replaced on Harper's head.

"I should have taken you away long before," Harper said softly.

"I was so caught up in self-pity and was afraid of the unknown," Hailey admitted.

"Unknown?" Harper glanced up at her.

"Our mother taught us one thing well—fear. We were so afraid of what was out there beyond our little hut that we didn't even consider leaving. We didn't think to tell anyone or ask for help," Hailey added.

Harper nodded and rested her head back on Hailey's shoulder. "I wonder a lot what would have happened to us if we'd been taken from her. If we would have been separated. That was the number one fear. The number one reason I kept my mouth shut."

"I never knew what Fred was doing to you. Not until after that last night," Hailey confessed.

"You were young. No one ever talked to us about those sorts of things," Harper said.

Hailey shook her head. "How can you be with Nick now and not"—tears rolled down Hailey's cheeks—"and not think back?"

She thought of the fear that ate at her each time she felt Reece's body against her own.

Harper hugged Hailey tight.

"It's different. Sex with someone you like or love is magical. It's like night and day. Do you like Reece?" Harper asked. Hailey nodded her head quickly. "Have you kissed yet?" Hailey nodded again. "How did it feel?"

Hailey was quiet for a moment as she thought of the feeling of Reece's lips against her own. "Magical," she admitted softly.

"Trust him. Trust yourself. The rest will be just as special," Harper said.

Hailey rolled her eyes as she felt her face heat. "It's sort of embarrassing." They had never had the sex talk. Their mother had never had any talk with them, actually.

"Life is embarrassing if you make it. Embrace yourself, sex, Reece, whatever comes next. Being with Nick has opened my eyes to all that was taken from us. The more I'm with him, the more I realize just how much we lost. And at this point, I want it all. Everything I never knew to dream about."

That sounded wonderful. Having the life she had always dreamed about. Being free to just... be. To live, laugh, explore, travel, have a career, to love.

Hailey hugged her sister tight. "I love you."

"I love you." Harper laughed as tears rolled down both of their cheeks.

Nick knocked on the door and opened it. Reece and Lucy were with him. Lucy jumped up on the bed and rushed to lay against Harper's side.

Hailey stood up and tried to hide the fact that she was wiping tears from her eyes.

"How are you feeling?" Reece asked Harper, but Hailey understood he was really asking her.

Harper hinted that she was tired, and she and Reece decided to head home.

As they left the room, Harper said to Reece, "Thanks for taking care of my sister. If you hurt her, I'll slap on my boxing gloves and kick your butt."

Reece smiled and nodded. Then he wrapped an arm around Hailey's shoulders and walked out.

Chapter Ten

They drove home in silence. He could tell Hailey was deep in thought and tired from the obviously emotional evening.

When he parked in the driveway, he realized that they had left her truck at Baked.

"I can drive you to work in the morning," he said, shutting off the truck.

"I've made up my mind," she said, turning slightly towards him.

He waited, removing his seat belt as she removed her own.

"Okay," he said when she didn't continue.

"I'd like to go to Vegas with you," she said with a slight smile.

He smiled quickly. "Okay. I'm leaving on the fifteenth, the day after Valentine's day, and returning two days later."

She nodded. "I'll ask for the time off." She turned to look at the house. "What about Ali?"

"Hannah is going to watch him."

She nodded and then turned back towards him.

"I've made up my mind about something else as well." She spoke so softly, he had to lean closer.

"What's that?"

"Us." She shifted and suddenly she was sitting in his lap, her mouth fused to his. "This," she said against his lips.

He would have liked to think that he wouldn't be so easily distracted from the previous topic, but this was sex and he was a man. And he'd been fantasizing about Hailey for over a year.

With all those factors, it was any wonder he could think at all. Facts were, however, facts. They were currently sitting in his truck in his driveway, which was not the place he'd dreamed of doing this with her for the first time.

"Let's go inside," she purred against his ear. She sucked on it and it felt like his eyes crossed.

"Yes," he agreed eagerly.

While she dislodged herself from him, he tried desperately to compose himself. They walked into the house, hand in hand.

When Ali bombarded them, he knew the dog needed a pee break and some attention. Sex was just going to have to wait.

"I'll let him out," he said, feeling his heart jump at the way Hailey was looking at him.

She nodded and, instead of heading up the stairs, she followed him and the dog through the house towards the back door.

"I don't want a moment alone to reconsider," she admitted when the dog darted into the backyard.

Just knowing she was second-guessing herself had him pulling her into his arms.

"If you have doubts," he started, but she stopped him by kissing him again.

"I don't have doubt that I want to be with you," she admitted. "I do, however, have doubts about how it's going to make me feel. You know my past. But I don't think you know yet that you'll be my first." She avoided his gaze.

He shifted his hold on her until he could nudge her chin up enough for their eyes to lock.

"First since...?" he asked. When she shook her head, he frowned.

"First ever. First one that I wanted." Her voice cracked slightly, and he waited until she took a deep breath. "If that night hadn't happened, you would be the only one ever."

He felt tightness in his chest and pulled her into a hug.

"That's a lot. It means a lot." He felt her nod in return. "We'll go slow. You let me know if I do anything"—he shifted until his eyes locked with hers again—"anything at all that scares you."

She surprised him by smiling. "I thought just talking about all this would be scary. Harper suggested I open up to you. Trust you." She lifted on her toes and brushed her lips across his. "I do trust you."

He almost melted just hearing those words from her.

The second the dog darted between their legs back into the house, he shut and locked the door, then he lifted Hailey up until her legs wrapped around his hips.

"Let's head upstairs," he said against her neck. He concentrated on not dropping her or bumping them into any walls as he went.

When they reached his room, he realized that she deserved candlelight and soft music. He'd promised her a first date and here they were about to take the biggest step in their relationship before they'd even really gone out.

The moment her body slid down his, her fingers tugged at his shirt.

His mind and body screamed to take her quickly, to find his release and pleasure. The rational part of his heart had him slowly stepping back from her reach.

"If we're going to do this, let's take it a step at a time." He turned down the light until it was low enough that it could be considered romantic.

He took her hand and led her over to sit on the edge of the bed. Then he knelt before her and slowly untied her shoes.

She sat still, watching him, smiling down at him. He took a moment to gently rub her feet, knowing she'd been standing on them all day at work. She groaned and arched her feet into his hands.

"You're good at that." She laughed when he hit a ticklish spot. He released her foot.

"I'm good at a lot of things," he teased as he slowly ran his hands up her legs. Then he pulled her to the edge of the bed until her body was pressed against his. His hands moved slowly over her hips, up her back.

He knew that she had issues with being held and, even though he'd moved slowly, he felt her tense against him. He stilled.

"Are you okay?" he asked softly.

She took a moment before nodding. "Yes, I..."

"Don't like being held down or held tightly?" he suggested. She nodded. "Want me to let go?" he asked as he started running his hands gently over her back.

She took another moment and then shook her head. "No," she said.

He felt her take another deep breath as her hands moved to his shoulders. He held still while she explored his arms, his shoulders, his chest.

"I like the feel of you," she said softly.

He wanted to tell her that she was driving him crazy. That if she kept it up, he wouldn't be able to contain himself for much longer. Instead, he allowed her to pull off his shirt this time.

One step at a time, he kept telling himself. Let her take the reins for a while until she feels comfortable again.

When she kissed him, he pressed his body against hers again and held in a sound of happiness when she didn't tense this time.

The more she took control, the more he felt her relax. But when he started unbuttoning her blouse, he could see her nerves and fears return. He kissed her as a distraction and once more had her relaxing.

When he stood her up to remove her pants, she nudged his off as well.

"I..." She bit her lip and avoided looking at anything other than his chest.

"You can look," he said with a smile. "Trust me, I am looking at you." He chuckled.

She jerked her eyes up and then down at herself.

Her matching blue bra and panties covered her like a second skin and were turning him on so much he didn't know how he was holding back.

Then her eyes slowly traveled down his chest, and he thought he'd burst with want.

"Hailey," he groaned when her fingers slowly traveled down him.

"I... like what I see," she said, jerking her eyes back up to his. "I want to see what you feel like."

He smiled and then motioned for her to continue. He held still, not even taking a breath while she traced over him. When her fingers brushed against his erection, he jerked.

"Sorry," she said, blushing.

"No, it's... I want to be gentle with you and go slow. If you touch me, I'll have a difficult time," he admitted.

"I've never wanted to touch a man before," she said as she ran her fingertips slowly over his chest.

He rolled them over until she was straddling him, then laid back and let her explore him as much as she wanted. It took all of his self-control not to take what he wanted from her.

When she stilled, he glanced up at her.

"Is... do you like this?"

He chuckled and nodded. "Make no mistake, you're driving me crazy."

She smiled, then gasped when he shifted again, this time laying her down on the bed.

"Tell me if I do anything..." He dropped off when she nodded in understanding.

Instead of covering her with his body, he knelt between her thighs, spreading them wide. With a smile on his lips, he moved down until he could run his mouth over her flat belly.

Her fingers dug into his hair, and he felt her arch towards him.

He couldn't keep the taste of her out of his mind and wanted more. Exploring lower, he slid her panties down until he exposed her, then he ran a fingertip over her.

She cried out his name in a half moan.

His eyes jerked to her face, concerned that she would tell him to stop. Her cheeks were flushed and her head thrown back, so he could tell she was enjoying what he was doing to her.

"Do you like this?" he asked her softly as he kissed the inside of her thigh.

"I... don't know. It's..." she started, but then he covered her pussy with his mouth, and she cried out and jerked under him.

He held her still with his hands on her thighs as he lapped at her, enjoyed pleasing her. Her nails dug into his head, holding him closer to her.

"Come for me, Hailey," he said against her. "Scream my name when you do." He trailed a finger over her, before dipping it into her heat while he took her clit into his mouth.

Feeling her convulse for him, hearing his name rip through the quiet house, made him smile, and he grew even harder than before.

Shifting, he pulled out a condom from the bedstand, then slid up her body and hovered just above her.

"There's no turning back for me now," he said with a sigh. "I couldn't stop wanting you if I tried." He kissed her. Her arms and legs wrapped around him, pulling him closer. When he slid into her for the first time, he felt as if he was right where he wanted to be for the rest of his life.

In the darkness, he listened to her light breathing. He'd pulled them under the covers to ward off the chill in the night air.

Ali was happily snoring in his dog bed at the foot of the bed.

Even though his body had cooled from the passion, his mind was still driving him forward, wanting her. Needing to know more of what she'd gone through.

"I need to tell you something tonight. I promised Nick and Harper I would," she said.

He was surprised that she was still awake.

"Okay," he said, his voice sounding deeper since he was relaxed and sleepy.

She shifted away from him and suddenly he was chilled at her absence.

When the bedside light came on, he shifted and watched her search around for her clothes.

"Do you have to be dressed to do it?" he asked with a chuckle.

She glanced at him, and he could see the weight of what she wanted to tell him in her eyes.

He nodded and climbed out of bed, understanding that this wasn't going to be a fast conversation.

"How about you head in and get something comfortable on while I go make us some tea?" he suggested, pulling on a pair of his sweats.

She gathered her clothes in her arms and left his room wearing only her panties and bra.

He slid on a shirt and, leaving Ali snoring, headed downstairs to make them some tea.

When Hailey came downstairs wearing a pair of gray yoga pants and a large T-shirt, he searched her eyes and knew she was nervous.

"Here." He handed her a mug of chamomile tea. She took it and sat at the bar, and he set some cookies that his mother had made for him on a plate in front of her.

She took one and took a bite. He sat next to her.

"I've told you that our mother was an addict," she started. He nodded, understanding that she would want to tell him everything without interruption. "Heidi's addictions were varied. Alcohol, heroine, prescription drugs. You name it, she did it." She took a sip of her tea and set the half-eaten cookie down. "A few months after my fourteenth birthday, Fred showed up at our place." She shifted in her chair and leaned back, her eyes moving to the dark windows that overlooked his backyard. "We were still in school, so we didn't see much of him. He would stick around for an hour or two, and he and our mother would get high or..." Her eyes turned to his. "I didn't know at that time why they would lock themselves in my mother's room for hours." He nodded in understanding. "He kept coming around. That summer, things progressed, and Fred moved into the house with us. I didn't know it at the time, but he was hurting Harper." She closed her eyes. "Raping her almost every night."

His tea jerked and he almost spilled it. He set the mug down and took a deep calming breath. She'd already told him that the man abused them both, but it was different hearing that it was a constant thing for such a long time. He wanted to kill Fred.

He was thankful that Hailey kept her eyes closed.

"Then, a week before my fifteenth birthday..." Her eyes opened and she turned towards him. "He came for me."

Chapter Eleven

Hailey tried not to remember that night. What Fred had done to her. Tying her up, gagging her, raping her. There are parts she blocked out, thankfully.

Then there are the other parts. The moments she plays over and over in her mind at the strangest times. Like in the middle of brushing her teeth or helping a customer.

Those seconds tick by, much like they had those long hours she'd been Fred's plaything, as he'd called her.

"He liked that I was a virgin. Back then, I had no clue what that was." She glanced at Reece, thankful that he was hiding his emotions very well. "Our mother was never there for us in any aspect of our lives. If it wasn't for Harper"—she shook her head— "I wouldn't have known the basics of being a teenage girl."

"This is the man after you? The one who attacked Harper tonight?" he asked in a strained voice.

She nodded. "Harper was worried when the news report of her and Nick saving those kids from the bus went national. She'd always feared he'd find us." Her eyes locked with his. "That last night, before we ran away, when Fred..." Her throat closed up for some reason, so she picked up her tea and took a sip of the now lukewarm liquid. "When I finally freed myself from the ropes he'd used on me, I crawled into Harper's bedroom. The gag was still in my mouth. I was naked," She closed her eyes and swallowed. She felt Reece's hand on hers and all those fears about the past just disappeared. She felt as if she could continue, as if the simple contact somehow made her stronger. "Harper untied me, helped me clean up, helped me dress, then she disappeared for a while. When she came back, we left and spent the night in the woods. The next morning, Harper went back to the house and told me to wait in the woods at one of our hiding spots. I didn't know why, but when she came back, she had a backpack of food and some cash. We hiked for a few days and then spent our first night in a motel. But first she stopped off at a drug store and..." She bit her lip, wondering if she had said too much. If Reece was going to kick her out and tell her that their night together was a mistake. Still, the look on his face had her finishing. "She used all our money and bought a morning-after pill for me."

Reece didn't even move. Didn't even blink.

"Harper said that, with her, Fred always used a condom. With me, that night, he hadn't. For the next few weeks, we went to the free clinic and I got tested. We don't trust doctors, well, Harper doesn't. Until tonight, she hadn't even been seen by one before." She shook her head. "But with me, it was different. I had no clue what STDs were or even really knew how pregnancies happened. I'm clean and clear of everything," she added quickly. "I wouldn't have... tonight, if..."

His hand tightened on hers. "I know. I'm clean too," he added. "Just so that's out there." He smiled.

She nodded, needing him to hear the rest. "Harper told me later that our mother had died that night from a drug overdose. She hid it from me for a few weeks. I can't remember when she finally told me, but I do remember not really caring much. I was glad she was gone. She was a terrible person. Part of me hoped that Fred was gone too." She looked down at their joined hands. How different they were. His were large, tan, strong, hers thin, shorter, smaller. "That first year, we traveled a lot. Motel after motel. Harper got jobs, most of the time serving drinks at some bar or strip club. We were in a motel just outside of Atlanta when Fred found us. Well, he bumped into Harper at work one night," she corrected. "Harper ran out of there, and we packed up and left Georgia. Over the next few years, we headed west. She didn't tell me about our great-uncle's place until we were outside of Vegas. At that point, we'd never spend more than a few months in any single town. She encouraged me to finish school and since I'd always gotten good grades, I took my GED." She smiled remembering how proud Harper had been. How they had celebrated that night with burgers and cupcakes. "Our uncle's cabin was the first real home we ever felt safe in." She turned her entire body towards his. "I won't let him take that away from us. I won't let anyone take that from us. Harper deserves to be happy. I deserve to be as well. Fred almost killed her tonight and instead of wanting to run and hide from him again, I want to kick his ass. I want to punch him so hard," She took a deep breath and realized Reece was smiling at her.

"You and me both. I think you can add Nick to that list as well. Along with a few other people in town that care about you two," he said.

She smiled. "I love Pride. Love the people in it. I won't let him take that from us."

Reece reached up and touched her cheek, and she realized he was wiping a tear from her face.

"If you keep up your training, you won't have anything to fear." He leaned closer and brushed his lips across hers. "I'm sorry you had to go through all of that. I can't pretend to understand the pain you've been through. But I want you to know that no matter what, I'm here. If there's anything you need to say, anything you are feeling, I'm here to listen."

She nodded. "Up until a few days ago, Harper believed she'd killed our mother."

"Okay," he said slowly. "Why would she think that?"

"When she disappeared, when I was packing my things, that last night at home, she snuck into our mother's bedroom and put rat poison in our mother's drugs. She said that Fred was sleeping on the floor, which made it possible for her to get to them. That next morning, when she went back, Fred was gone and our mother was... dead," she said slowly.

"What happened a few days ago?"

She nodded. "Nick found out her time of death from the official report. It was noted in the autopsy that she'd died the evening before. Before Fred... before. Before Harper had poisoned the drugs."

He nodded that he understood.

"For years, we've been running because we both believed Harper was a murderer. That if the police ever caught up to us, she would be locked up, and I'd be taken away from her. Even after I turned eighteen, we just worried that we'd be separated."

"She's your world," Reece said with a smile.

Hailey felt more tears roll down her cheeks. "She's everything."

He pulled her into a hug and she held on, realizing that it was the first time she'd ever opened up to someone other than Harper. The fear of being shamed or judged disappeared the moment he pulled her close.

Everything was changing. Her and Harper's worlds were changing. Her sister had Nick, loved Nick. She held in a sound as she realized that the two of them would probably get married. That was the next step, right?

That would, no doubt, leave Hailey all alone in the cabin. All alone in life.

"Hey," Reece said, pulling back a little. "What do you say we stop by tomorrow on your lunch break and make sure she's okay? We can bring her a pie, and you can see how she's doing."

She nodded, suddenly feeling drained. "I'm tired."

He stood up and took her hand and led them back upstairs. Ali was snoring in the middle of the bed, which made her smile. The dog was still small now, but someday he would probably push Reece off the mattress.

"He normally doesn't sleep on the bed," he assured her as he tried to get the dog to move.

"It's okay. Lucy sometimes sleeps in bed with me." She crawled under the covers and pulled Ali close to her. "Where are you going to sleep?" she joked.

Reece climbed in behind her and pulled the pair of them tight against his chest. "There, this is where you both belong."

She wanted to agree with him, but there was an odd lump in her throat. She remained quiet and replayed the wonderful night she'd just had over in her mind until she fell to sleep.

The next morning, Reece had to take a phone call and headed downstairs to let Ali out while she showered and dressed for work.

When she went downstairs, he had a bagel with pecan cream cheese and a mug of coffee ready for her.

"I know you're heading in early for inventory this morning," he said after he kissed her. "So I made you a quick breakfast and coffee to go."

"Thank you." She took a sip of the coffee and held in a groan.

"I'll see you in a couple hours. I have a few things to catch up on here first." He answered another call.

Once every month, she helped Carter out with inventory. When he'd found out she was interested in how Baked ran, he'd started letting her help with some of the business tasks.

She loved inventory. Loved bookkeeping.

Carter joked that she had a twisted mind like he did because they both were thrilled when inventory time came around.

Just before lunch, Reece showed up and they ordered a few pizzas and headed to Nick's place.

Her sister looked tired but happy, and Hailey sat watching her while she ate.

"Fred went to the Edgeview hospital last night after attacking me. He got thirteen stitches on his arms and had a broken finger. But they released him before the APB went out," she told them.

"So we know for sure it was that son of a bitch?" Reece said, glancing at her.

Harper's eyebrows rose slightly.

"I told him everything," Hailey said, touching her sister's arm.

Harper nodded. "Nick knows everything as well. I think Tom does too, but..." She shrugged.

"What happens now?" Hailey asked them both.

Harper sighed. "Now we wait until he makes another stupid move. I think he knows we're not staying at the cabin any longer."

"Right." Hailey nodded. "Does that mean he's going to leave the cabin alone?"

"Tom and Nick are stopping by twice a day to check up on it. To make sure he's not destroyed anything else." Harper leaned back, looking even more tired than before.

Just then, Nick returned from picking up Blue from the vet. The dog had saved her sister and lost part of his ear in the process. He'd also lost his manhood, as the vet had neutered him while he was there. The poor dog had a cone around his head. When he saw Harper, however, he perked up and sat by her sister's side until they left.

Returning to work, Hailey felt suddenly drained.

There was no guarantee that Fred wouldn't go after Harper again. No way to stop him from coming after her.

Both Carter and Corey knew that she was scared of a stalker. Nick had talked to them, and they'd agreed to keep an eye out for the man and protect her. She was never alone in the restaurant anyway. She'd locked up a few nights, but Carter or Corey was always there.

Since her shift had started early, she left just before the dinner rush. Reece had stuck around after lunch, working in the back booth on his laptop for a while before heading home.

Parking next to him in his driveway, she wondered how long it would take for Fred to leave them alone.

Reece was there to open her truck door and help her get out.

"I was thinking," he said, pulling her into a hug, "it's about time I introduced you to my world." He wiggled his eyebrows.

"Your world?" she asked, but his chuckling stopped her, and she understood he was talking about his father's business. Video games.

They'd had a few discussions about the game Modark, since her sister had asked what he did for a living. She was curious about it and nodded.

"We'll make sandwiches and head downstairs, I have the game set up on the big screen down there." He wrapped his arm around her shoulder.

"What are you going to do when I kick your butt?" she joked.

He laughed. "Honey, I've been playing Modark since I was two. There is no way you're going to kick my butt." He stopped just outside the door and smirked at her. "Unless you cheat."

Chapter Twelve

How in the hell was Hailey winning? He wondered if subconsciously he was letting her win. Then he focused really hard on the game and was still behind in points and precious life beans.

What in the hell?

"Are you sure you've never played this before?" he asked for the tenth time since they'd started the game.

"I've never played any video games before," she said, not taking her eyes off the screen. Then she slammed down another magic fruit and upped her score even more.

"Ugh," he groaned, searching around the field for more berries or magic fruit. Instead, he tripped over a toadstool and lost life beans. "Shit." He smiled when he remembered a shortcut to a bean stash.

"That's cheating," she said when he tripled his bean count.

"What? Just because I wrote the code doesn't mean it's technically cheating," he said as he watched his score go up even more. He was still behind her, but at least he wasn't losing by hundreds.

"You'd better watch out. My pixie is going to cast a spell on your Watchman," she warned, seconds before his character turned blue. Suddenly, his controller stopped working and Sidlyk the Watchmen, the character he normally played, started following her pixie around as if she was his owner.

"Damn it." He set the controller down. "Best two out of three?" he said as she made Sidlyk do cartwheels. She laughed.

"This was by far the most fun I've ever had," she said, setting her controller down.

"I should have started you out playing my normal game. Sidlyk is a level-fifty Watchman in that game, not a measly level one like your pixie."

"Don't be a sore loser." She nudged his ribs. "My pixie will gain more powers, just wait and see." She leaned back on the sofa. "She just needs more training."

He leaned back with her and let their shoulders touch. Their sandwiches and chips had been devoured hours ago, before they'd gotten lost in the competition of the game.

"Oh, and what about Hailey?" He shifted, pulling her up over him until she was looking down at him, smiling. "How much training is she going to need to be powerful enough to make me follow her around and do cartwheels?"

She ran her hands through his hair and then leaned closer and whispered in his ear.

"Something tells me it won't take much, other than a promise of a repeat of last night."

He felt his entire body go rigid as his mind replayed the evening before.

"Damn, you're probably right." He groaned as he ran his hands over her body. "We could head upstairs now and…"

"No, here, now." She covered his mouth with hers. "Please."

It was the please that did him in. The soft way her voice almost cracked as her hips moved over his.

He would have given her anything. Hell, he would have done cartwheels if she'd ask him to at the moment.

Then she surprised him by leaning back and quickly removing her shirt. The white bra underneath was like a beacon in the dark room.

The scene of his character flipping upside down was frozen on the television.

When she started unbuttoning her jeans, he moved to cover her hands and take over the task for her.

Slowly, he helped her remove each barrier on the both of them. When they sat there completely naked, her eyes boldly ran over him.

She was standing in front of the television set, nothing more than a dark silhouette. His eyes took in her curves, how wonderful she was.

So much had changed in her in such a short time. She was growing bolder, stronger, more exciting.

He slipped on a condom and wiggled his finger at her.

"Come here, sit on me," he said, motioning to his lap.

She hesitated for a moment, then took a step closer.

He guided her to where he wanted her, where he knew she would be the most comfortable.

"Slide down on my cock," he said between kisses. Her fingers tightened in his hair.

"How?" she said against his lips.

He took her hand and helped her grip him and then guide him inside of her.

The moan of pleasure she released as she slid fully onto him matched his own.

"Wow," she said as she arched back.

He took her face in his hands and waited until her eyes locked with his. "Now ride me."

Her hips started moving, slowly at first, then faster when she lost herself in pleasure.

Feeling her convulse around him, seeing her eyes change as she was consumed with her release, was like magic. There was no stopping his own release moments after hers.

Cartwheels came in all different forms, he thought to himself as he held her.

When Valentine's came around, he thought about what to do. Normally, he would ask a woman he was dating out for Valentine's dinner, but Hailey was scheduled to work that night.

Even though he couldn't take her out for dinner, he could still do something special. He swung by All in Bloom and picked up a large bouquet of multicolored flowers. He made a mental note to ask Hailey what her favorite color and flowers were.

Walking into Baked with a large bouquet of flowers was a little awkward. That was until Hailey walked out of the back room and saw him.

The way her face lit up was well worth the few moments of embarrassment.

"Are these for me?" she asked after rushing across the room.

"Yes." He nodded and hugged her and then, in front of everyone in the restaurant, he kissed her until his heartbeat spiked.

He thought he heard a few people sigh and clap, but he

was too preoccupied enjoying the feeling of Hailey softening against him.

"Happy Valentine's Day," he said, giving her the flowers. "There's something else." He motioned towards the card on the flowers.

She pulled the flowers up to her face and smelled them. "I've never gotten flowers before." She hugged them to her chest.

"Then I'll make it a point to get them for you often," he promised. "I didn't know your favorite color or flowers."

"Blue," she answered quickly as she opened the card. "My favorite color is blue. My favorite flower..." She frowned slightly. "I've never thought about it." Then she smiled at him. "I like these." She ran her fingertip over a soft white carnation.

"That's a carnation," he said as she silently read the card. "You're taking me on a date in Vegas and giving me money to gamble?" she asked, sounding exciting.

He nodded. "I didn't know what else to give you. So I figured, while we're in Vegas, I'd take you gambling. You said when you were in Vegas last time, you never got to."

She hugged him. "Thank you. I can't wait for tomorrow." She smelled the flowers again. "Now, however, I had better get to work." She laughed.

"I can order us dinner. I figured we could at least eat together. Carter says you can take your break when it comes out." He motioned back towards her boss, who waved and gave them both a thumbs-up.

Hailey chuckled and then kissed him again before disappearing to the back room with her flowers. When she came out again, she rushed around serving food and refilling drinks until their dinner was ready.

He'd chosen to go with the chicken parmesan instead of ordering their usual pizza.

While she'd been working, Corey had shuffled to the booth and set a candle down on the table. "At least we can set the mood a little," he said with a wink before disappearing.

Reece liked the brothers. When they'd first moved into town, they'd been well received. It had taken him a while to figure out which one was which. The twins were identical in almost every way. Now, somehow, he could tell the pair apart, even when they dressed in the same uniform and styled their hair the same.

The only other adult twins he knew were Riley and Jacob, and they were as different as night and day. Sarah and Parker Clark had twins, Ethan and Ellie. They looked a lot alike, but most children did until they grew older.

He wondered if Hailey liked kids. He'd grown up around children and most of his friends now had families of their own. He couldn't imagine that she and Harper had been around a lot of kids, considering how they were raised.

He watched her across the room as she joked with customers and then she knelt down to pick up a crayon that their child had dropped. She talked to the kid softly and then tickled the little girl's cheek before leaving the table.

He thought about what he wanted. He'd always hoped for a large family. There hadn't been a time when he hadn't wanted at least four kids. He'd loved being raised with his older sister, but he'd always wanted a younger sibling or two.

He kept thinking about kids until she finally set their food down in front of him and joined him in the booth.

"Wow, this is one of my favorite meals here." She took a drink of her tea. "How did you know?"

"I've seen you eat it before. The look you get on your face says it all." He wanted to tell her the look was a lot like the look she had when he pleased her, but there were kids running around, so he decided to keep that to himself.

Instead, he touched her cheek and leaned in to kiss her before they ate.

He knew she had to get back to work soon after they were done with their meal, since the restaurant was packed. He wanted to prolong their time together, but at least they were set to leave first thing in the morning to fly to Vegas. He kissed her goodbye and gave up his table. There was a line of people waiting to be seated.

When he got home, he took Ali on a long walk, then decided to strap on the gloves and work out for a few hours.

He was in the best shape of his life. Still, he knew how important the coming fight was to his career. He had to do his best and be better than the guy he was fighting. Robert Carrigan Jr. had won more than a half dozen fights in the past year.

Reece had won his last fight, but that had been a little over a month ago. He'd cancelled a few after finding out about Hailey's stalker. He'd wanted to stick close to home to help keep an eye on her.

He was sure he could beat Robert, but still, he stayed down in his gym until his muscles ached and his fists were raw.

Then he took an ice bath followed by a shower until everything was numb.

When Hailey got home, he was sitting at the kitchen table, double-checking their flight and hotel reservations.

He'd never stayed at the Aria in Vegas before and went online to check out the room his agent had booked for him, the Sky Villa, a two-bedroom two-story suite that looked amazing.

Then he looked for the perfect place to take her out to dinner and booked them a reservation at a nice restaurant within walking distance to their hotel.

On a whim, he booked them a couple's massage for the next morning. He'd still have plenty of time before the fight to take her gambling.

The fighting ring was set up in one of the Aria's main event centers. The fight started at eight that evening. It was scheduled to be shown on several sports channels.

It was the largest fight he'd been booked in so far and, if he was being honest, he grew a little anxious when he thought about being in front of a crowd so large.

Then again, he knew that once he stepped into the ring, nothing could tear his focus away from the match.

When Hailey stepped into the house, his heart skipped a few beats.

Damn. She was going to be there, front row, watching him. How was he going to concentrate with her watching him?

Chapter Thirteen

Hailey had never been on an airplane before. She would have been nervous, but she kept replaying the special conversation she'd had the day before while helping Harper do her hair for her date with Nick.

She was going to be an aunt. Harper and Nick were having a baby.

Her sister was going to be a mom. As excited as she was for her sister, one question weighed heavily on her.

Where did that leave her?

Sure, things were going great with Reece. But she knew that the moment Fred was caught, she would be returning to the cabin. Alone.

Reece had only invited her to stay with him because she was in danger. Would he want her to stay longer? That was doubtful.

There was no question that he was enjoying her sleeping with him each night in his bed. She enjoyed being with him more than anything else in the world. When they lay together, her dreams were filled with the life they could make together. But since she'd never dated anyone before, she figured she was jumping too far ahead, pushing things in the relationship further than his intensions.

They'd only been sleeping together for a few nights at this point. Their first official date was going to be that night in Vegas.

Her mind returned to the flight when the plane bumped slightly. When she'd told Reece she'd never been on an airplane before, he'd taken her hand and assured her it was going to be fun. The moment they sat down, she realized something was different.

First, they'd been seated before anyone else. Second, their seats were in the front of the plane.

It dawned on her when the steward handed her a mimosa after Reece had asked for two drinks.

"Are we in first class?" she asked him in a whisper.

Reece smiled. "Yes," he whispered back. "Do you like it?"

She glanced around. "Yes, but I have nothing to compare it to."

"Well, for starters, you won't get these back there." He held up his glass and waited for her to hold up her own. Then he tapped the glasses together. "We'll get breakfast too before everyone else. We board first and have bigger seats."

She nodded. "Okay, so far so good."

The rest of the flight, he filled her in on what he had planned for their trip. She thought he kept talking to keep her from being nervous. It worked.

When they landed, she was so relaxed and excited for the next step in their journey, she didn't even flinch when the plane bumped to a stop.

From there, they made their way out of the airport. She

was thankful they'd only packed small suitcases so they didn't have to wait to get their luggage.

After stepping out of the airport into the warm desert air, they walked down to where a black car was waiting for them. The driver put their luggage into the back of the SUV, and Reece helped her onto the cool leather seats.

She watched out the window as they made their way onto the Strip and headed towards their hotel.

The last time she and Harper had been in Vegas, they'd stayed at a homeless shelter for a few nights before Harper had gotten a job and they'd moved into a motel far outside of the city. Hailey had wanted to get a job, but they hadn't stayed long enough for her to find one.

When they pulled in front of the Aria hotel, she felt her heart kick with excitement. She had never stayed somewhere so nice before.

"Wow," she said more than two dozen times as they checked in and were shown to the elevators.

"You keep saying that." Reece chuckled as he took her hand in his.

"It's a little overwhelming," she said with a sigh as the elevator doors shut. "I mean, I don't know where to look. There's so much to take in."

He pulled her into his arms. "Remind me to take you to Rome and the Vatican someday." He kissed the top of her head.

"You've been?" she asked, feeling her heart jump. She'd read a book long ago about Rome and the city within. She'd studied the pictures for hours and hours.

"When I was in high school, our folks took us," he answered. "You haven't been outside the States?"

She almost told him that the only reason she had a copy

of her birth certificate was that Harper had requested copies so she could get her GED. She didn't even have a passport.

She shook her head. "Nope. Someday I hope to go. I've always wanted to see to see the Coliseum."

"Maybe we can go together," he said as the elevator doors slid open.

The door to their room was open and while Reece talked to the man who had carried up their bags, she stepped inside and held in a gasp.

There had to be some mistake. This wasn't a hotel room. It was a full-blown apartment.

A massive two-story gold staircase in the shape of a twisted S sat in the middle of a huge space. A wall of windows looked out over the city, and a comfortable-looking L-shaped beige sofa, two blue chairs, and a large glass coffee table sat off to one side. On the other was a dining room complete with a table that could sit a dozen guests.

"Well?" Reece said, moving over to wrap his arms around her.

She was standing by the windows, looking out at the view far below them.

"I know I've said this before, but wow." She turned in his arms and hugged him. "Does your agent always treat you this well?"

He chuckled. "Nope, only when I'm headlining. Shall we take a look at the rest of this place?" He motioned towards the stairs.

She laughed and they held hands while they explored the two-bedroom suite.

Downstairs was a full kitchen, dining and living rooms, and a powder room that was easily double the size of the bathroom Nick and Harper had just remodeled in the cabin.

Up the golden staircase were two main bedrooms, each with their very own massive bathroom. Each one had a circular jetted bathtub in the middle and a glass shower that could fit an entire football team in it. The bedrooms were gorgeous and slick in design with modern furniture and neutral colors.

It was more than she could have ever dreamed up.

"What do you want to do first?" he asked after moving their luggage up to the bedroom they'd chosen to sleep in. "We still have a few hours before our dinner reservation."

"Shopping," she suggested. "I saw some stores in the lobby area, and I'd like to see about getting a dress for tonight." She took his hand and pulled him towards the stairs.

He laughed and followed her out. They walked back out to the elevators.

He was a really good sport as she tried on several dresses in the shop in the lobby area.

Finally, she settled on a gold-sequined spaghetti-strap dress that went with the gold heels she'd packed for their dinner. She found a little clutch bag that went with it and ended up spending far more than she'd intended.

"I have a confession," she said as headed back to their room almost two hours later. "I love clothes."

He laughed. "I figured as much. My sister used to drag me to the mall in Edgeview all the time."

"You were a really good sport about it. All those stereotypes of men hating shopping." She waved her hand. "I don't believe them."

"Oh, it's true. My father would rather have needles poked in his eyes than to go shopping with my mom and sister." Reece laughed.

They both stopped dead in their tracks when they noticed the huge poster by the entrance to the casino area.

There, in full color, was a huge picture of Reece, shirtless, in boxing gloves and shorts, facing another man who was looking angrily at Reece. Reece had a face of determination rather than anger. The banner had the details of the next night's fight and boasted that tickets were sold out already.

"What in the..." She rushed over and stood in front of it. Then turned to him as he moved to stand beside her. "Wow, that's the man you're fighting?" She pointed to the angry-looking man.

"Yup, Robert Carrigan Jr." He wrapped an arm around her. "His father was a legend in the boxing ring."

"He's massive." She frowned at the image of the larger man.

"No, the poster only makes him look bigger than me since I'm the nobody." He tilted his head. "Actually, I'm about a foot taller than he is. He has muscle on me, though. That's the reason I've been bulking up the last month."

"You're going to be okay, though, right?" she asked, glancing at him. "You'd tell me if you were scared."

He nodded. "For sure."

Suddenly, someone squealed behind them and a group of women rushed towards Reece.

"You're him," they said, stumbling on their stilettos while their tight skirts rode up high on their thighs. The way the women pawed at Reece while they asked for pictures with him in front of the banner had a wave of jealousy washing over her.

Hailey had never been jealous before and didn't quite know what to do about it.

For the next few minutes, Hailey stood back while the

group took many photos and one woman even live streamed for a while and did a little interview with Reece. Afterwards, she kissed Reece on the lips "for luck."

Reece jerked back slightly when the woman stopped kissing him and looked over towards Hailey as the women walked away.

"I'm sorry," he said, taking her hand. "I had no clue she was going to kiss me."

She shrugged. "I know. I could tell. You looked very uncomfortable."

"She tasted like vodka," he admitted, then made a show of wiping his lips clean. He surprised her by leaning her over backwards and kissing her until she forgot all about the group of women that had practically pawed him moments earlier.

"Let's head upstairs and get ready for our date," he said when he stood her upright again. Taking her hand in his, she strolled back towards the elevators, passing three other banners with his image on them as they went.

"They must have just put them up," he said when the doors shut. "I don't remember seeing them on the way to the shops."

"We took the other hallway," she pointed out.

"Right. It's sort of embarrassing. Seeing yourself that big."

She chuckled. "And half naked. That part I didn't mind. Do you think they'll let you keep one? I took a photo, before your groupies arrived." She glanced down at her phone. She'd also gotten a few shots of him posing with the women, just to show Harper when they got home.

When they got to the room, they were surprised to see a man standing outside their door, looking down at his phone.

"That's Aaron Hunt. My agent," Reece said before the man turned towards them.

"There you are," the man in the expensive-looking suit said as he rushed to shake Reece's hand. She noticed the man quickly assess her and dismiss her. "Tell me you packed a suit?" Aaron said quickly.

"I did." Reece nodded. "We were just about to get ready for dinner."

"Nope. Sorry, dear." He waved his hand towards her. "I need to steal my star for a few hours. We have cocktails with investors in half an hour, followed by more cocktails with event bigwigs, followed by dinner—"

"Sorry, can't," Reece interrupted the man. "I'm taking Hailey out. We have reservations." He unlocked the door and motioned for Hailey to step inside.

Aaron followed them in and didn't even glance around the room. Instead, the man turned on Reece.

"Reece, baby, if you want to make it in this world, you have to wine and dine as well as jab and knock out." Aaron slapped Reece on the shoulder.

"I'm having dinner with Hailey," Reece asserted.

"Bring her with." Aaron waved his hand as his phone rang. The man answered the call and walked away, then threw over his shoulder, "We leave in half an hour."

Reece turned to her. "We don't have to—"

"It's okay." She wrapped her arms around him. "We'll go. You have to do what you have to do." She leaned up on her toes and kissed him. "Which means we had better get ready quickly." She released him and headed up the stairs.

Half an hour later, they walked down the stairs, her in her new gold dress and Reece in a black suit. He looked sexy as hell.

She wished they had time to admire one another, but Aaron was waiting.

"Good," the man said when he spotted them. This time, the guy's eyes ran over her as if he was seeing her for the first time. "Good," he said again with a nod. "This will do nicely." He tapped a few things on his phone. "Your name?" he asked her.

"Hailey," she answered as Reece wrapped an arm around her.

"Hailey what?" Aaron asked without looking up from his phone.

"Davis," Reece answered for her. "Aren't we going to be late?"

Aaron continued to type on his phone and when he was done, he smiled up at him. "It appears the two of you are already making waves." He turned his phone around and showed them an image of them kissing in front of the banner downstairs less than an hour before.

One of the women that had taken pictures with Reece had obviously snapped the photo when he had kissed her.

Hailey was bent backwards, her arms wrapped around Reece's shoulders as they were locked in the kiss. They had both been so lost in the kiss they didn't realize someone was taking the picture. The poster of the fight was perfectly framed behind them, as if they had posed between the two fighters on purpose.

She instantly wanted a copy of the image for herself.

Chapter Fourteen

"It's all over social media. Everyone wants to know who your love interest is, and I just answered that million dollar question." Aaron took his phone back from Hailey. "Now, we're late."

Reece had known the man for long enough to know there was no use in arguing with him. Whatever Aaron had planned, it was important to comply.

Taking Hailey's hand in his, he followed Aaron out of the room and into the elevator. While the man was busy with another call, Reece leaned closer to Hailey.

"Are you okay with this? I can tell him to go to hell," he whispered.

"No, really, I can tell this is important," she whispered back and then kissed him. "Really," she added.

He felt like an ass. He wanted a romantic evening with her, alone. To show her what a real date could be like. After all, there were so many things she hadn't done before. Airplane rides, dates, playing the slot machines, massages, and so much more that he wanted to explore.

When they stepped outside the hotel, Aaron guided

them to a massive limo. Hailey whispered to him that she'd never ridden in one before. One more first.

As the limo darted in and out of traffic, Aaron filled him in on the night's events.

First stop was to a nightclub, where they were set to meet some of his sponsors for a drink or two. Aaron quickly ran through a list of people that were waiting to meet him.

While Reece tried to keep each name in his head, he could tell that Hailey was enjoying the limo ride. He wished that he'd thought to offer her a drink of the champagne that had been chilling when they'd climbed in, but the limo was slowing and pulling in front of the nightclub. He'd make sure she had a drink inside.

He should have had some flowers delivered to the hotel. He would make sure to do it the next morning.

He helped her out of the limo and followed Aaron through the doors without stopping by the two very large bouncers holding the doors open for them.

Aaron walked to the back of the club like he owned it and sat down behind a bright pink rope in a massive booth that was directly next to the crowded dance floor. There was a DJ on stage at the front of a sea of bodies that were bouncing up and down with the fast rhythm.

He pulled Hailey down next to him and waved the waiter over to order her a cocktail of her choice. By the time their drinks arrived, the first of the sponsors had arrived, and he and Aaron were busy chatting with them.

He wanted to pull Hailey out onto the dance floor. To feel her body brushing against his. To enjoy the night. Instead, he tried to keep focused on work.

Several times he did reach over and take her hand in his. She seemed to be enjoying watching the crowd and listening to the music.

Then again, she probably wouldn't tell him if she wasn't enjoying herself. He knew she'd made up her mind that, whatever happened on the trip, she was just happy to be there.

The truth was, he was even happier that she was there with him.

After the first sponsor left, he leaned over and told Aaron he was going to take Hailey out onto the floor until the next sponsor showed up.

Aaron nodded as he looked down at his phone.

He took Hailey's hand in his and pulled her up to her feet.

"Dance?" he said as the music slowed. Perfect timing, he thought. When she nodded, they stepped out onto the floor and directly into the middle of the crowd of people.

Feeling her in his arms sent a wave of joy through him.

How had she become so important in his life? He could no longer even imagine not having around. What had he ever done without her? How had he lived before her?

"Did I mention how wonderful you look?" he said next to her ear.

"At least a dozen times." She sighed and wrapped her arms around his shoulders. "You look dashing in your suit. Sexy." She ran a finger over his collar.

He smiled. "I wish we could just leave here and head back to our hotel room."

"Me too," she purred, and then she lifted on her toes to kiss him. "But it appears your next meeting has arrived." She motioned behind him, and he glanced over and groaned.

He took her hand and led her off the dance floor just as the song ended and the beat sped up.

He shook the older man's hand and waved for another round of drinks.

By the fourth meeting, Reece had had enough. He could tell that Hailey was getting drunk since every time someone new arrived, another round of drinks was delivered.

She needed food.

"How many more?" he asked Aaron.

The man glanced down at his watch and then his phone. "Two."

"Hailey needs some food."

Without answering, Aaron raised his hand and spoke to the waiter.

Moments later, a basket of chips and salsa were set in front of Hailey. She gladly started eating the chips like it was caviar instead.

This was not how he expected the evening to go.

Still, Hailey looked so sexy in the little gold dress and heels that it was almost impossible to keep his eyes off her.

When she disappeared to find a bathroom, his eyes followed her the entire way. Excusing himself, he met her in the hallway when she came out of the bathroom and kissed her until they were both breathless.

"Later, I'm going to make this up to you," he promised her softly as he laid his forehead against hers.

"Okay." She giggled and pressed herself against him one last time.

When they made it back to the booth, he stilled when he saw the next man he was supposed to meet with. He knew him. Hell, everyone in the boxing world knew him.

Half of the people on the dance floor had stopped to take photos of the boxing legend sitting in the booth waiting to meet him.

"Is everything okay?" Hailey asked beside him.

Reece took a deep breath and nodded. "Do you know who that man is?" he asked, nodding towards the booth.

Hailey glanced over and shook her head. "Should I?"

"That's William Billy Cox," he answered, half holding his breath.

"Who is...?" Hailey asked.

He smiled and leaned down to kiss her. "Only one of the biggest boxing heroes, who I've idolized my entire life." He led her to the booth.

Reece's hands trembled as he shook the man's hands for the first time. He had to work hard not to stumble over his words as he introduced Hailey.

For the next half hour, he gushed all over the man, who seemed just as excited to meet him. William talked about Reece's stats as if he knew them by heart. It shocked and happily surprised him that the man knew so much about his career. He was a nobody in the boxing world.

When the man stood up to go, he pulled Reece aside as they shook hands.

"Make sure you look out for yourself. This world can bury you quick. It can take the people that are important to you and push them aside. Don't let it." He turned and gave Hailey a hug and told her how nice it was to meet her before leaving.

"He was nice," Hailey said as she touched his arm.

"Yeah," he said, feeling a lump in his throat. "Damn, I didn't get a photo."

Hailey smiled and held up her phone. "I got about a dozen of them." She showed him her screen.

There were images of him and William shaking hands, leaning in towards each other, talking, laughing, and shaking hands again as they looked towards her.

He hadn't even seen her take them. They were perfect. She was perfect. He pulled her in and kissed her.

"You're perfect," he said, holding her.

"Last one before we need to head across town," Aaron said, motioning towards his next meeting.

Two men in expensive suits walked towards the booth. As they went, they pushed the dancers and other guests aside as if they were flies.

Reece immediately grew annoyed.

His emotions quickly went from happy to angry when he watched a woman stumble after being shoved aside.

"Easy," he told the men as he moved to help the woman.

Aaron laid a hand on Reece's arm. "Step down," he warned in a low tone.

The shorter man that followed the bodyguards was as well-known as William Billy Cox, only the man wasn't a boxer. Amos Bernard owned at least three casinos and hotels along the Vegas Strip.

Rumors said he was the head of an underground mob that went back several generations to his great-grandfather, who owned one of the first casinos in Vegas. The man was into a lot of things. Drugs. Women. Guns. Boxing.

Reece knew better than to make an enemy. No doubt the man standing before him had pulled a few strings to meet Reece tonight.

Tucking Hailey tight by his side, he held out his hand to the man and greeted him between clenched teeth.

He could tell that Hailey understood to keep in the background of this conversation. With William, she'd laughed and joked right along with them. Now, however, she sat next to him and smiled politely when Amos joked about her or Reece.

Thankfully, Amos and his two bodyguards didn't stay long. When the man stood up, Reece and Aaron did to.

"I look forward to watching you fight tomorrow." The man shook his hand. "I've got a cool mil on you, so don't disappoint," he added, pulling him in close.

"Jesus," Reece blurted out. Why in the hell would a man bet a million dollars on him?

Then Amos burst out laughing. "Just kidding." He smiled and then jerked his arm again. "I only bet a hundred thousand on new guys." He winked at him and then blew a kiss at Hailey. "Bring your good luck charm to the fight. I'll make sure she has a front row seat next to me." He wiggled his eyebrows.

"I think she's safer sitting next to my parents," Reece said.

Amos paused for a second, narrowing his eyes, and then burst out laughing again. "I like you. You're going to go far." He slapped him on the shoulder and walked away, following his goons, who were once again pushing the crowd back for him.

"That was... interesting," Hailey said when they were alone. "Was he some sort of mob guy?"

Reece and Aaron both laughed.

"Some sort," they both agreed.

Chapter Fifteen

Hailey was in a daze as they made their way out of the first club and were once more shuffled into the limo.

While Aaron and Reece chatted about the meetings they'd just had, she took a few photos of the inside of the limo and herself holding up a glass of champagne that Aaron had poured for them. She sent them, along with a few images of Reece and William, to Harper.

Earlier, she'd sent her sister pictures of their hotel room and the dress she'd bought for that night.

Harper responded with the image of her and Reece kissing in front of the poster.

"It's all over social media. They are calling you two the 'It' couple of the boxing world," Harper texted back. "Have fun. Be safe. I doubt that Fred is active on social media, but keep your eyes out."

When the limo stopped, she was shocked to see a large group of people standing outside of the nightclub.

Before she could see what was going on, the door to the limo opened and Aaron stepped out. "Well?" he turned and said to them, "the show continues." He wiggled his eyebrows.

Reece climbed out and then turned back and held out his hand. "Once again, I'm sorry for all this," he said.

She laid her hand in his and smiled up at him as he helped her out of the limo. She was thankful for his help since she'd had four drinks and only a bowl of chips at the last place. She wasn't hungry yet but thought about drinking a soda or water at this place just to level herself out.

She opened her mouth to respond, to tell him that it was okay, but bright lights exploded in front of her as people shouted. She had to blink a few times to see as people shouted their names while taking pictures of them. Reece's arm wrapped around her waist as they made their way through the crowd.

They were guided past the long lines and straight to the doors of the club. Once they stepped inside, the bright camera flashes and the sound of people shouting their names were replaced by disco lights and loud music.

The place was so crowded that she felt a little claustrophobic. They followed Aaron through the mob of dancers to a wide hallway and up some dark stairs that led to a smaller room. A low table sat in the middle of a massive circular booth in bright red leather. There was an unhindered view of the stage below them, where the band was playing to a full room of people.

"Wow," she said as she sat down on the leather seat.

"Yeah." Reece chuckled beside her. "Drink?" he asked when a waitress stepped up in front of them.

"Juice," she told him and he nodded. "Chips or bread if they have any."

After they had ordered, a group of people came into the

room. Hailey couldn't hear over the loud music as they were all introduced. She assumed the older couple, dressed in very expensive club attire, had something to do with Reece's boxing match. A younger couple, around their own age, who were also dressed in fancy club attire, came in a few moments later, and Hailey got the impression they were related to the older couple.

Instantly, Hailey was thankful she'd purchased the gold dress. If she'd worn the simple black dress that she'd packed instead, she would have looked and felt too simple.

The last person to arrive was a single man who looked bored and annoyed that he had to be there. She did, however, hear his name perfectly when he shouted it in her ear after she asked him.

"Bryce," he said in a British accent. He instantly lit up a thin cigarette and ordered a scotch. Then he sat on the other side of Reece and proceeded to monopolize his attention for the hour or so they were there.

She tried to hold a conversation with the younger woman, whose name was either Milly or Nelly, over the loud music. From what Hailey could understand, the woman was excited about the fight.

After another round of drinks, everyone stood up and made their way out of the club. They were shuffled into a bigger limo all together.

Here, at least, she could hear the woman's name, Nelly. Her husband, Carl, was the owner of the fighting venture that was sponsoring the fight. The older couple were Carl's parents, Carl Sr. and Robyn, the original owners of BVE, Boxing Ventures and Events.

Bryce was providing some of the money behind the next night's event and was apparently a Lord of some sort.

They stopped at another massive hotel and walked

through the lobby to the elevators. They got off on the top floor and stepped into the restaurant, which had a full view of the city below. They were seated in a private room off the back with a wall of glass doors that went out to a balcony.

Reece took her hand under the table and squeezed it as he leaned closer and whispered, "I guess this is nice. Still, I can't wait for our first date where we can eat dinner alone."

"We've eaten dinner alone plenty of times," she reminded him. "How often will we get to have dinner with strangers?" she pointed out, causing him to chuckle.

All through dinner, the topic stayed on the fight. Occasionally, she was asked a question, but for the most part, she chatted with Nelly about living in Vegas and their two children, ages eight and four.

Nelly was an ex-ballet dancer who had gotten a job as a Vegas showgirl after an injury ended her career in New York.

She'd met Carl Jr. after a show that she was in and the pair fell head over heels in love before she'd found out that he was the boss's son.

Hailey wanted to hear the entire story, but the dinner wasn't that long. Still, she got enough of the story to tell that the couple had endured the wrath of his parents for the first few years of marriage. It was only after their oldest child was born that they were finally accepted. After their second child was born, Carl Sr. let his son take over the family business.

In the past four years, the son had proven to his parents that he had a head for business. Tickets had sold out weeks before. This fight was going to be a success, no matter the outcome.

Somehow, knowing this, Hailey felt more at ease. Sure, she wanted Reece to win. She supposed it was an ego thing.

Her ego, not his. He was seeming to have fun no matter what. The way he looked at the entire ordeal as an adventure made her fall even harder for him.

If he had taken everything too seriously, she would have wondered what he would be like in other stressful scenarios.

When they left the restaurant, there was no limo waiting for them. Everyone headed out in different directions. Reece pulled out his phone and got them a ride back to their hotel.

"That was a night," Reece said with a sigh when they were in the backseat of the car heading towards the Aria. "I'm really sorry that our date got hijacked."

"It's okay, I enjoyed it anyway." She leaned into his shoulder. She'd drunk enough fancy drinks that she was feeling buzzed.

Being with him was somehow magical. She felt like a fairytale princess who had just met her Prince Charming.

Then again, the entire world was spinning at this point.

"We're here," Reece said softly, and she suddenly realized the car had stopped moving.

He helped her out of the car and they made their way through the lobby. They were stopped a few times by guests that recognized him. This time, instead of stopping to take photos, he politely told them he had to get to his room to rest up for the big fight.

Once they were in the elevator alone, Reece pulled her into his arms.

"Just how buzzed are you?" he asked into her hair.

"Just enough that it feels like we're floating. You?"

"I drank water all night," he said, surprising her.

"You did not." She slapped at his shoulder and missed, causing him to chuckle.

"I think a glass of water will help the headache in the morning," he said, helping her out of the elevator.

She sat down on the edge of their bed and he handed her a large glass of ice water, which she drank it down quickly.

"Better?" he asked, sitting beside her and taking the empty glass.

"I'm not thirsty for water anymore," she purred. She hiked up her skirt and straddled him, then kissed him until she felt dizzy again.

"Hailey, I'm trying to convince myself that you're not too drunk," he whispered while she nibbled on his ear.

"I am too drunk, but that doesn't mean I don't know what I want." She leaned back and looked into his caramel-colored eyes. God, he was so sexy. Sexier than any man she'd ever imagined being with. Not that she'd spent much time imagining it. Until he'd come along, she hadn't wanted any other man. "And I know one thing for sure—I want you. Now." She kissed him. "Drunk or not, I need you." She kissed him again until she felt him cave to her demands.

Being with him was a feeling she wanted to hold onto forever.

"Don't ever let go," she told him as his arms wrapped around her hips.

"I love the feel of you," he said as his hands slipped up her hips and around her back to squeeze her butt.

She groaned and inched closer to him until she was pressed tight against him. There had been a time in her life when she had feared men because of what one of them had done to her all those years ago for several horrible hours.

With Reece, none of those memories played in her mind. Only good things circled her thoughts as he touched her, kissed her, pleased her.

He made her body respond like it never had before. Bumps rose all over her body when his mouth moved over her skin and when his tongue dipped into her. She couldn't stop herself from shouting his name as he filled her.

While they lay in the massive bed, wrapped around one another, she shifted until she could look down at him.

"I've never said this to a man before," she started. His hand moved to her bare hip and stilled as he looked up at her with curiosity in his eyes. "I am so thankful you know how to make me scream your name," she finished with a smile.

He laughed. "I like it. I think I could spend forever hearing it." He pulled her back down and hugged her. "I'm sorry about our date being ruined."

"It wasn't. It was the most perfect date I could have ever asked for. I got to meet a Lord, one of your heroes, and a mobster." She chuckled. "How many other women can say the same for their first date?"

"You are amazing." He shifted until they were side by side and looking at one another. "You have this childlike outlook on everything. Every new experience is like finding a gold nugget, no matter if it's good or bad."

"Life is much better than it used to be," she said as he brushed a strand of her hair. "Finding you was the best thing to happen in my life."

His hand stilled. "I feel the same." He leaned in and kissed her.

She wanted to tell him more of her feelings but was afraid it was too soon. She didn't know the etiquette of relationships. Didn't know what the rules were. She'd never dated anyone before.

Sure, she'd watched plenty of television shows in the past few years that depicted how couples admitted their feelings. Right now, none of the advice she'd gained from reruns seemed to fit the situation. So she remained quiet and drifted off to sleep in his arms.

Her dreams were filled with the perfect life she never thought she'd have. The one she never knew she wanted. Life filled with Reece, Ali, Robin, Nick, her nieces and nephews, and children of her own.

Someday she just knew that life was going to come. Someday.

Chapter Sixteen

Reece woke long before Hailey did. He quickly sent out an order to have flowers and breakfast delivered to their room and waited for them to arrive downstairs.

After the table was all set with the large vase of flowers and the warm meal, he tiptoed back upstairs, climbed into bed, and kissed her until she woke.

"Morning." She sighed and held onto him.

"I have a few surprises for you this morning," he said with a smile. "Two of them are waiting downstairs."

Her eyes opened a little wider. "Coffee?"

He chuckled. "Yes, that too."

Taking her hand, he pulled her from the bed, and they walked downstairs together.

She gasped when she saw the table. "Wow, all this?" She walked over and buried her face in the flowers. "These are my favorites," she said as she smelled the soft blue carnation petals.

"I remembered." He held out the chair for her to sit and

when she did, he pulled off the cover to her meal. Then he poured her a cup of coffee.

"This is so amazing," she said when he sat down next to her. "I've never gotten room service before."

"Today we're going to do a bunch of firsts. After breakfast, we have a couple's massage booked."

"Really?" She practically jumped out of her chair. "Where?"

"They'll come here, to our room. I didn't know if you'd like your nails done." He glanced down at her fingernails and smiled at the soft pink color she'd painted on them. "So, if you don't want the service..."

"I do," she said quickly. "That's another first." She smiled and bounced on her chair. "Oh my gosh, you're spoiling me."

He lifted her hand to his lips and kissed her knuckles. "I like seeing your smile."

"I feel like I need to do something special for you," she said after she took a bite of her breakfast.

"You are. You're here. What would I have done in this place if I'd come alone?" He frowned. "I would have been bored, watched television, ordered room service and, did I mention, be bored."

She chuckled. "Well, then, I'm glad I could help out."

"After we're done being pampered, we can spend a few hours downstairs in the casino."

Her smile grew. "I'd almost forgotten. I get to gamble this time. I can't wait to get started."

"We have time," he told her with a laugh when she started eating faster. "Our appointment is in half an hour."

"That soon?" she gasped. "I have to shower and shave." She glanced at her watch as he laughed.

A little over half an hour later, after she had indeed

rushed upstairs and showered, they were lying face down on the massage tables in a massage room off the main living room that he hadn't even known was there.

He'd had a lot of massages in his life, and was enjoying relaxing, but he kept stealing glances at Hailey to see if she was enjoying herself as well.

When it was time for her to get her nails done, she moved into a chair as the nail technician started on her fingers while another started soaking her feet.

"I'm going to head up and take care of a few things." He leaned over and kissed her before heading out.

She looked well rested and excited about getting so pampered. She deserved it.

Every vacation his family had taken, his mother and sister had always booked a mani-pedi. He'd grown up knowing it was something women loved and enjoyed.

That he could provide Hailey's first experience of it made him happy.

After showering off the massage oils, he pulled on some clothes and called his mother.

"So, how did she like the massage and mani-pedi?" she asked upon answering the call.

"She's loving them. Thanks for the idea."

His mother squealed. "The two of you looked so cute last night. The photos are everywhere online."

He rolled his eyes. "Yeah, I guess I didn't realize that I'd be pulling her into the spotlight with me."

"Your dad and I are going to be there in a few hours. Do you want us to meet you up in your room?"

"No, we're going to hit the casino floor in a bit."

"Oh good. I'll text you when our flight lands. We're almost ready to board now."

"Hey, son," his father said loudly, causing him to chuckle. "See you in a few hours," he said and hung up.

He knew he probably still had time before Hailey would be done downstairs and logged onto his computer. Sure enough, several images of them from the night before were everywhere on social media.

When he googled the fight, images of them in the clubs showed up, and he realized that Aaron had probably hired a photographer to follow them around.

Some of the pictures were so good that he saved them to his phone.

"What's this?" Hailey said over his shoulder.

"Us." He glanced up at her.

She looked happy and relaxed, and he pulled her into his lap and showed her the images. "Apparently Aaron had a photographer follow us around. Either that or we had a stalker." He winced when he remembered her situation.

Thankfully, she was too engrossed in flipping between the images to mind his faux pas.

"These are amazing." She stopped at the image of him and William and smiled. "You look like you have stars in your eyes." She laughed.

"I did." He held her tight. "How about you shower and get dressed, and we'll head downstairs to spend some money at the tables? My parents flight gets here in a few hours. They're going to meet us on the floor. The three of you can have some dinner while I head in to deal with all the pre-fight details. Then you can go over to the fight together."

"What should I wear?" she asked, standing up.

"Whatever you want. It's pretty casual downstairs, but for the fight but I wouldn't say no to seeing you in that dress you wore last night." He wiggled his eyebrows at her as she laughed.

"I think I might have something that you'll like." She disappeared into the bathroom.

He did a few searches on his opponent for the night, Robert Carrigan Jr, who had spent the night before drinking and partying at another Vegas nightclub with a string of women on his arm.

Compared to those photos, Reece looked like a saint. The man was obviously living it up while in the City of Sin.

Would that help him win the fight? He knew that the boxer had a string of doctors on hand to make sure he was in top shape.

Reece was in top shape too. Better than he was last year at this time. The time he'd spent close to home had helped him focus on his health, diet, and training. He was more than ready for the fight.

When Hailey came out of the bathroom wearing a tight pair of black leather pants, spiky-heeled boots, and a sequined white shirt with only one shoulder, he almost lost his breath.

"How does this fit?" she asked, turning around.

His mouth watered.

"Hello?" she asked, moving closer to him, his eyes locked on her body.

"I think I'm in trouble," he admitted.

"Oh?" She walked over and wrapped her arms around his shoulders.

"How am I supposed to concentrate on the fight when you're wearing this?" he asked, running his hands over the smooth material over her hips.

She chuckled. "Easy, I'll be sitting down. "Next to your parents," she whispered.

He laughed and then kissed her.

"Take me gambling," she said against his mouth.

"Yes, ma'am." He stood up quickly.

He watched her face the moment they stepped onto the casino floor for the first time. To him it was noisy, crowded, and very overwhelming.

The smile on her lips told him it was nothing short of magical to her.

"Where do we start?" she asked, her eyes darting everywhere.

"First, we get some credits. They used to just give you coins of your choosing, depending on which machines you wanted to play, but now you get casino cards. We can get chips for the tables if you want to try those first."

They found the cashier, and he got them each a card with a hundred dollars on it. "It's a start," he told her. "We can get more put on if we want."

"A hundred is more than enough." She placed the card on her wrist with the clips provided.

"No, you don't want to do that." He took it off and handed it back. "It's an easy mark for thieves."

She nodded and slid it in her front pocket. He did the same.

"The first rule of gambling is"—he leaned closer to her—"drinks." He smiled.

"You're going to have water." She tilted her head. "I think I drank enough last night."

He nodded. "They have virgin drinks."

"Oh, a daquiri would be great then." She glanced around. "Where's the bar?"

"In casinos, they deliver them to you." He took her hand and they made their way through the floor. "Let's start with something small." He found the quarter slots and after they each found an empty machine, he showed her how it worked.

Before someone arrived to take their drink orders, she had already won an extra hundred dollars while he was down ten bucks.

"You're very lucky," he told her when there drinks finally arrived. "I'm down while you're up"—he glanced at her machine and shook his head—"almost two hundred."

"This is fun." She laughed when she won again. "I could do this all day."

"You wouldn't be saying that if you were losing," he pointed out.

She stopped to take a drink. "You're probably right. I don't really have the money to spend to keep going." Then she laughed. "But for now, I have extra money that I can enjoy." She motioned to the machine.

They sat at those machines for a little over an hour. When her winning streak dried up, they headed to get lunch at one of the restaurants before making their way to the tables.

Hailey liked roulette the best. She picked it up quickly and, here too, she won while he was down almost his whole hundred.

Since he was having more fun watching her than gambling himself, he sat back and enjoyed the show.

By the time his parents showed up, she was up almost eight hundred dollars. His folks had checked into their own room and changed for the evening.

His mother always looked great but her Vegas attire was, no doubt, the reason his father had a big smile on his lips.

It was interesting watching her interact with his folks. They'd known each other for over a year. From everything his parents had told him, they liked Hailey and her sister very much.

His parents suggested they sit down for drinks and catch up, so they made their way to the bar area.

He had never really felt comfortable with his parents around someone he was romantically involved with before. Whenever he'd brought a girl home, he'd been so nervous.

Now, however, he couldn't help thinking how right this was. How at ease they all were, as if they knew it was a perfect fit.

When he got a call from Aaron telling him he had less than an hour before he had to get ready for the fight, he kissed Hailey and said his goodbyes to his parents.

"One more for luck," he said and kissed Hailey until he felt their hearts beat together.

"You're going to do great," she told him, cupping his face.

He wanted to tell her that he loved her. The desire to say those three words was so strong at that moment that he even opened his mouth. Then he realized that he could do better than blurting it out in front of his folks, so he shut his mouth and rushed away.

This too felt right. He was going to find the best time to tell her, to show her, how he felt about her.

Chapter Seventeen

Hailey felt nervous. Not because Reece's parents, Luke and Amber, were sitting across from her. No, the only reason she felt nervous was because Reece was walking away from her and she wanted more than anything to blurt out that she loved him.

Her palms grew sweaty and her heart raced each step Reece took away from her.

"He's going to do great," Amber said, touching her arm.

"I know." She sighed and realized that there would be better times to admit her feelings for the man who had stolen her heart.

"He's got this," Luke added. "Carrigan is a little crazy, but our son has a calmness about him that the Carrigan boy doesn't. Reece will wait for the perfect moment and"—Luke swung his arm as he smiled—"knockout."

"You think Reece will knock out Carrigan?" Amber turned to her husband. "Since we're in Vegas, care to make a little wager on that?"

Luke laughed. "You're on."

Hailey watched the older couple flirt, but instead of feeling awkward, she found it all very amusing that two people who had been together for so long still acted like they had just fallen in love.

She'd never had a couple as a role model. She didn't know what marriage should or could look like. Sure, there were movies and television shows. One of her favorites after they had left home was *Everybody Loves Raymond*.

Although the show had been funny, it really hadn't given her a clue as to what loving someone really meant. This, sitting across from her, was a far better example than any actors could portray.

This was real love. Something she believed she felt for Reece.

After they left the bar area, they decided to head back to the tables. Since she was up almost nine hundred dollars, she sat at the blackjack table and had Luke teach her the ropes.

He quickly lost fifty bucks while she gained thirty.

Gambling was fun, but she did wonder if she would be having as much fun if she was losing, like Reece had pointed out.

Since they still had an hour until they had to take their seats for the fight, they decided to get something to eat.

It was amazing how comfortable she was around his parents. They laughed and joked about Reece and Hannah's childhood. She listened to stories about how the sister-brother duo used to play jokes on one another.

She knew firsthand how close Reece was with his sister. She and Harper were just as close, so she understood perfectly.

After dinner, they made their way down several long hallways. It wasn't hard to figure out where the fight was taking place, as the walls were covered with pictures of Reece and his opponent.

The hallway led into a massive room. They rode the elevators down to find a sea of people waiting in line.

Amber gasped. "Do we have to wait in that?"

"No, Aaron said he'd meet us at the private entrance." Luke looked around and then motioned towards the side.

Aaron was standing just outside a doorway, looking down at his phone. When he spotted her and Reece's parents, he perked up.

"There you are." Aaron shook Luke's hand and then hugged Amber. "How was your flight?"

"Good," both of them answered.

Then Aaron turned towards her and hugged her. "Good to see you again."

The man had practically ignored her the night before. Suddenly, he took her arm and started leading them through the doors as he handed Luke a couple of passes.

"Here's yours," he said to Hailey and then stopped in a dark hallway and helped her put it on over her head.

She wondered why he was giving her a bunch of attention all of a sudden. She supposed it was due to all the images of her and Reece everywhere.

When they stepped into the massive empty room and she saw the ring in the center, she felt a wave of excitement rush through her.

Reece was in the ring talking with a group of men. He wore a long black silk robe with his name on the back.

"I made that for him." Amber smiled as they moved closer. She'd grabbed her other arm, which thankfully forcing Aaron to drop his hold on her since the aisle was too narrow for three people to walk side by side.

"He looks so serious," she pointed out.

Amber chuckled. "He has always been able to concentrate on the sport. To him, it's as important as when he writes code for Modark." She shook her head. "He gets that from his father. I have ADHD." She sighed. "It seems like yesterday he was wearing diapers and chewing on his sister's fingers." She chuckled then lifted her phone and took a picture of Reece.

They were shown to seats along the front row. "These are yours," Aaron said just as his phone rang.

Suddenly, Reece glanced over in their direction, and she saw his concentration slip as his eyes landed on her. His smile was quick, but she felt what it did to her deep in her core. Her body had an automatic response to him. Would it always be like this? She hoped so. Hoped they had many years to come together.

She sat down and watched as the men continued to talk quietly. When they were done, Reece headed towards them and climbed out of the ring, followed by a few of the men, and stopped in front of them.

She and his parents stood. He wrapped his arms around her, then pulled his parents in for a group hug.

"I'm heading back until the fight starts," he told them in the huddle. "Thanks for being here for me."

She didn't know what to say, so she let his parents talk to him, encourage him, praise his skills.

He stood back then leaned in and kissed her quickly before leaving.

"He's going to do great," Amber said as she wiped some tears from her eyes. "I'm so proud," she added when Luke pulled her into a hug.

"Of course you are," he said with a smile.

For the next hour, they sat in their seats while other people shuffled into the arena.

When the place was almost full, the lights dimmed slightly.

"We still have half an hour," Luke pointed out. "If you ladies need to hit the bathroom, now is the time."

"I should go." Amber stood up. "Hailey?"

"Yes." She thought she could make it but knew that, once the fight started, there was no way she was going to stop watching it for a bathroom break.

She and Reece's mother made it back down the aisle, this time wading through the people heading towards their seats. The bathrooms were situated outside the main door to either side.

She followed Amber to the closest one and stood in line with about half a dozen other women who had apparently had the same idea.

They chatted about the wonderful morning she and Reece had and what their plans were for the next day, before their flight left in the evening.

Reece's parents were staying on for another couple of nights before heading back home.

She wished that they had more time in Vegas but knew that she had work the day after they were set to return home.

After using the bathroom, she washed her hands and stepped out of the crowded bathroom and into the hallway to wait for Amber.

"You're her, aren't you?" someone asked, getting her attention. "Reece's girlfriend." The woman stopped in front of her. "Yes, it is you." She smiled then held up her phone and took a photo of her. "Can I get a picture with you?"

"Uh, sure." Hailey chuckled and then posed with the girl who was standing in line.

After that, she felt awkward and stepped further away

from the line while she waited for Reece's mother to come out.

She was standing in front of one of the large posters of Reece when hands wrapped around her, and she was pulled back into a dark side hallway.

"There you are, Princess," a man hissed in her ear. "I've got you now."

Her entire body froze at the sound of Fred's voice and his nickname for her.

It was as if every thought, every method Reece had taught her to defend herself, just left her brain. Instead, images of what Fred had done to her that night so many years ago played in her head like a rerun.

His hands gripped her tighter as he pulled her further down the hallway.

"I knew I'd find out where you went. All it took was searching for that boyfriend of yours. The bastard's going to pay for touching you. You're mine, all mine now, Princess," Fred said as he continued to pull her further into the darkness. "Your bitch sister has protected you for the last time. I'll get rid of her soon enough. She kept you from me for too long."

When they got to a fire exit door, he kicked it open. Instantly, the alarm sounded, shattering the daze that she was in.

Her body reacted. The moves Reece had taught her, the hours they had spent perfecting her ability to get away from a man who was easily double her size, kicked in.

Her elbow jerked into his ribs and her fist rammed up into his nose.

Seeing the fresh bandage on his finger and remembering Nick telling them that he'd broken it, she grabbed the finger and twisted until Fred's screams echoed in the hallway and she felt his finger pop in her hand.

"Hey!" someone shouted and then a blur rushed towards Fred and knocked him away from her. "Run!" Amber looked at her, but she didn't budge, so Amber took her hand and yanked her back down the hallway until they stood just outside the bathroom doors with a group of women.

"Is she okay? I saw the man grab her," the woman Hailey had just taken a photo with said, rushing to their side. "Gosh, it's a good thing I saw him grab you and screamed."

"Are you okay?" Amber said, breathless.

Hailey stood there, shocked and still as everything that had just happened replayed in her mind.

Her eyes moved to the hallway. She held her breath, waiting for Fred to appear and rush after her again.

"He's not coming back," Amber assured her as she wrapped her arms around her. "I saw him run out the fire door."

Just then, a group of security personnel came over to them.

"Who opened the fire door?"

While the group of women and Amber filled them in, Hailey was shown to a chair and handed a glass of water.

Had that really just happened? Had she just escaped Fred? Had he come all the way to Vegas to kidnap her?

His words played over in her head.

"I knew I'd find out where you went. All it took was searching for that boyfriend of yours. The bastard's going to pay for touching you. You're mine, all mine now, Princess."

"Reece," she gasped, the first words out of her mouth since the attack.

"He's okay," Amber assured her. "I think..." She took a deep breath and then took her hands. "I think it's best we tell him what happened after the fight."

Hailey thought about how big of a distraction it would be for him. Hell, he'd probably want to cancel the fight and head out to hunt for Fred himself.

Nodding, she stood up.

"Feel better?" Amber asked.

Hailey nodded again.

"Good. I'm going to call Tom and Nick so they can have a chat with the Las Vegas police so everyone can keep an eye out for that man. I assume it was Fred?"

Hailey nodded once more. "He said that he found me by all the photos online. He found me because of Reece."

"Don't stress about that right now," Amber said after a moment. "I think you need a shot of something strong." She narrowed her eyes. "We'll hit the bar on the way back inside. We'd better hurry, the fight's about to start. Are you okay?" she asked again.

Hailey mentally checked out her entire body. Nothing was hurt. The man had grabbed her, but nothing more than Reece had done when they had been sparring.

"I'm good. You? That was a pretty impressive fly tackle that you did back there," she pointed out, feeling proud at how the small older woman had taken down the giant of a man.

Amber laughed. "I learned from the best. My son," she added with a wink. "Come on." She took her hand and led them to the bar area. "If we aren't in our seats by the time Reece enters the ring, I fear the outcome of this fight." She laughed. "He loves you, you know that, right?"

Hailey, still halfway in a daze, nodded.

Yeah, she did know that. There was only one question in her mind—did Reece know how she felt?

Chapter Eighteen

eece was used to pre-fight jitters. What he wasn't used to was the sheer size of the venue he was fighting in.

After all the technicalities were dealt with—weigh-ins were mainly just for show at this point—he sat in a back room that served as his locker room and chatted with Aaron and a few other men who followed him around during the entire process.

He didn't stop to ask their names and really didn't care. He was pumping himself up so he could do what he needed when it came time to fight.

When Amos Bernard and his two bodyguards strolled in, he held in a groan.

"There's my boy," Amos said, slapping him on the shoulder.

"Evening, Mr. Bernard." He shook the man's hand.

"So, how are you feeling?" The man ran his eyes over him.

"Ready to fight," he assured him.

"Good, good." The man tilted his head. "You make sure you take out Carrigan in the fifth round."

Reece chuckled. "I'll try."

Amos smiled. "There'll be an extra ten grand for you if you do." He slapped him on the shoulder again and then walked over to chat with Aaron.

Reece sat down again and wondered if the man was being serious.

He was making bank on the fight already. Twenty-five thousand for a fight he would have paid to be in. More if he won. To him, the sport was something he enjoyed more than the win.

It wasn't as if he needed the money either. To him, the challenge was what mattered. He wanted to see if he could take the guy out in the fifth round more than he cared about getting paid to do it.

After that, there was a parade of investors, the ones he'd met the night before. He'd never felt so on display as he did at that moment. The fact that he was only wearing his boxing shorts and the silk robe his mother had stitched his name in made him feel completely unprepared for the visits.

He was almost mentally exhausted by the time he was ready to walk out into the arena. He had to pump himself up and take a moment in the hallway to close his eyes and breathe until he felt settled back into place.

Thoughts of Hailey floated in the back of his mind, the life he hoped he'd have with her after all of this. When they'd return home together, see his dog, take long walks, continue just being with one another every night.

He loved her. There wasn't a doubt about that anywhere in his mind.

To him, the next steps would be to slowly convince her to marry him. Raise a family together.

He'd witnessed his parents living their happy-ever-after lives, and so many other couples in the small town were also stupidly happy together.

It was a Pride thing. Everyone in town knew that the majority of townsfolk found love and stuck with it.

The divorce rate was so low in the small town that George Stevens, one of his buddies who was the town's primary lawyer, boasted that he'd only had three divorce cases since returning home and opening up his practice.

He could see him and Hailey being happy together. Forever.

Still, part of him questioned if she felt the same powerful feelings for him that he had for her.

Did she want marriage in her future?

Since the night she'd opened up to him about her past, how her mother and her mother's boyfriend had treated her and Harper, not once had she hinted she wanted any sort of future with him.

Maybe she was afraid of commitment?

She talked a lot about going back to the cabin once Fred was caught. Talked about how happy she was for Harper and Nick and that the cabin would seem empty without her sister.

Was that her way of telling him that whatever this was between them wasn't as deep for her as it was for him?

He had to clear those doubts from his mind. Had to focus on the fight. He knew that the moment he stepped into the ring, his mind would automatically clear and focus.

If he didn't think about these things now, he might end up making the wrong move later.

Saying I love you to someone meant a lot. To date, he'd only ever said those words to his family. Now he was thinking of telling the woman who'd trusted him with her darkest secrets.

By the time Reece headed down the long hallway into the area, he was certain that sharing his feelings with Hailey was the right choice, and that tonight was the right time.

The moment he stepped into the area, the entire room erupted with cheers. This was bigger than anything he'd ever done before. Something told him it was bigger than anything he'd ever do.

When he climbed into the ring and held up his fists, the cheers rose as his eyes moved over to his family.

He paused on Hailey's face, thinking for a moment that it was paler than before. Then she smiled, and he relaxed and smiled back before turning to greet his opponent. It was easy to push everything in his mind other than the fight to the side.

His thoughts sharpened when Robert Carrigan Jr. approached him.

The entire room was charged with an electric energy as the crowd grew silent in anticipation of the two fighters meeting.

When the spotlight focused on them, standing face to face, Reece held out his gloves to the man as the referee made his pre-programed speech about having a clean fight and went over the rules.

Carrigan ignored Reece's gloves until the ref was done, then he hit them hard and strolled away to cheers.

Reece returned to his corner and waited for the signal to start the fight. Reece was determined and, even though Carrigan was a formidable opponent, the man didn't really know his strength and resilience.

When the first bell rang, he focused on remembering

the moves that Carrigan used, the skills that he repeated when he was struggling.

The first round was a wash. He doubted either of them scored any real points.

He'd taken a couple blows and given a few in return.

He purposely avoided looking towards his family. He couldn't afford to be distracted. Instead, he kept his eyes on Carrigan, watched for any sign of weakness.

The guy looked winded by the end of the second round. Reece was positive he was up in points. He'd gotten in more solid hits and one that had caused Carrigan to wobble on his feet.

But Reece knew that he couldn't afford to get cocky. At any moment, the fight could easily turn in Carrigan's favor.

In the fourth round, he was on defense. The man had overwhelmed him a few times. Still, he hadn't taken a solid hit yet. He knew that he had to change tactics.

The fifth round he dominated. He had four solid hits and the fight had to be paused while they assessed a cut on Carrigan's eye. The man was wobbling.

Reece was growing tired of dancing around, so he figured he'd go all out before the end of the round. Besides, he really liked the idea of the bonus Amos had offered him.

It was now or never, he thought as he waited for the right moment.

When the bell rang, signaling the continuation of the round, Reece moved swiftly, his footwork precise and his guard up. Carrigan, a powerful figure with a menacing glare, advanced with calculated steps. The atmosphere was tense, every spectator holding their breath, waiting for the explosive clash.

Reece's focus on his moves was so intense that nothing

else mattered. His hearing was blocked, his vision and mind were only on Carrigan and his next moves.

Reece jabbed with speed, landing quick punches just under Carrigan's guard. Carrigan absorbed the blows, showcasing the durability he had become famous for. The crowd erupted with cheers as Reece danced around just out of the reach of Carrigan's return blows. Carrigan, however, retaliated with a powerful hook that just grazed Reece's cheek.

Reece easily brushed the blow off and thought through his moves as he waited for his next opportunity.

Reece's strategy was clear—quick, precise strikes to outmaneuver his opponent. Carrigan, on the other hand, relied on his brute strength, aiming for knockout punches. The man's muscles meant he could easily out-power Reece.

As the round progressed, Reece's strategy began to pay off. His speed and agility allowed him to evade Carrigan's powerful punches, while he landed a series of effective combinations. The crowd's excitement reached a fever pitch as Reece unleashed a devastating uppercut that rocked Carrigan.

Sensing his opportunity, Reece continued to press the advantage. But Carrigan weathered the storm and retaliated with a thunderous right hook that momentarily staggered Reece. The ebb and flow of the fight intensified, each of them giving their all in pursuit of victory.

In the final moments of the round, Reece dug deep, summoning his remaining strength for a final flurry of punches. A rapid combination culminated in a powerful left hook that sent Carrigan sprawling to the canvas.

Everyone always assumed that his right hook was his most powerful move. Up to this point in the fight, he'd held back his left. So when he finally pulled all his power and took the man down with one final left hook, everyone watching was in shock.

The entire arena erupted, then grew silent when Carrigan quickly stood up. The man wobbled around as the referee made his way towards him. Before he could reach him, however, Carrigan fell face first onto the mat, and Reece knew the fight was over.

The referee began the count, and when he reached ten, the bell rang, signaling the end of the match.

Reece stood victorious in the center of the ring, sweat streaming down his face as he basked in the cheers of the crowd for a few seconds.

The boxing ring, once a battleground, now transformed into a symbol of sportsmanship and dedication. The cheers for his victory sounded so much sweeter than those that had come before.

For those few seconds, it was the best moment of his life.

Then, pain shot through his chest and side. The blow lifted his feet from the mat and threw him backwards.

He landed hard on the mat, looking up at the bottom of the scoreboard, wishing more than anything that he could look at Hailey one last time as everything grew dark.

Chapter Nineteen

The entire room burst into sheer and utter chaos when the first gunshots echoed in the crowded room.

"Reece!" his parents screamed at the same time while Hailey stood there, dumbfounded at what she was seeing.

One moment she and everyone else in the auditorium had been celebrating Reece's victory. The next, they were unsure of what had just happened. They watched as Reece was thrown backwards onto the mat and blood flew out of his chest. Then more shots sounded and all hell broke out.

She was shoved, pushed, and pulled away from the ring. Then someone took her hand and pulled her back towards it, as if rescuing her from a tidal wave dragging her out to sea, away from where she wanted to be, needed to be.

"We have to get to him," Amber said, trying to shove her way back to the center of the room.

Hailey helped push them back to where Luke was kneeling over his son, shielding him from any more bullets. His hand covered his son's chest as red blood oozed slowly between his fingers.

Reece's eyes were shut and he had an odd color to his face.

"He's shot," Luke said to Amber, who cried out. "Someone shot him." His voice cracked slightly.

Another man approached them and yelled over the chaos that he was a doctor.

Luke helped the other man put pressure on Reece's chest while a group of people surrounded them as if using their bodies as shields.

She was surprised to see that Robert Carrigan Jr. was one of the ones locking arms to protect the man who had just beaten him in the ring.

She knelt next to Amber and held onto the woman as they worked on Reece. Finally, a few officers showed up with some EMTs, who put Reece on a gurney.

They were shuffled quickly out of the arena, down dark hallways, and stuffed into a car that followed the ambulance holding Reece in it.

"Why?" Amber kept crying as she held her. "Why would someone shoot my baby?"

Luke's phone rang as they pulled into the hospital. "It's Hannah," he said, shaking his head as if trying to clear it. He answered the call.

She could tell from Luke's side of the conversation that Reece's sister knew what was going on.

"It's all over the news. She's been trying to call us," he explained.

"I must have left my purse in my seat," Amber admitted.

Hailey realized that the only reason she still had hers was that she had strapped it crossways over her shoulders earlier.

"Let me talk to her." Amber took the phone when Luke handed it to her.

When the car stopped, they climbed out and rushed into the hospital while Amber continued to talk to Hannah on the phone.

Amber was telling her that, no, they didn't know who had shot him. No, they didn't know his status. Yes, he was alive, breathing, and no, it didn't appear that he'd been shot in the heart.

Hearing those words caused Hailey to break. Her body crumpled in the front desk area as she was consumed with guilt and sorrow.

Hands held her, lifted her, held her as she cried harder than she ever had in her entire life.

Even after being tied up, raped, and beaten, she hadn't cried as hard as she did now.

"Hailey, honey, we have news," Amber said sometime later, softly shaking her out of the darkest place she'd ever been.

She jerked her head up and realized it was Luke who was holding her like a child while Amber sat next to him.

"He's in surgery. They say the first bullet hit him here," She motioned near her collarbone. "The second one hit him in the ribs here." She touched her lower left side. "The doctor is very hopeful. His vitals are good. He's very healthy." She smiled and nodded a few times as tears rolled down her cheeks.

"This is all my fault," she said softly, suddenly too tired to think. Her head hurt from the tears, from the worry, from the pain of knowing this was her fault.

"Honey, no," Amber started.

"When he attacked me, he told me Reece was going to pay. I... I didn't think..."

Luke tensed under her.

"When who attacked you?" Luke asked.

Thankfully, she didn't have to explain anything since Amber quickly relayed what had happened before the fight.

"Shit." Luke stood up, then placed Hailey in the chair. "I'll be right back." He took his phone from Amber.

"We should have told him," Amber said with a sigh. "I should have told him." She leaned her head down. "I was just so caught up in the fight. I thought we'd have plenty of time after... I didn't know he'd threatened my son."

"This is all my fault," Hailey said again. "I... I didn't know he'd shoot him. I..." She cried and then was pulled into a hug. "I'm so sorry."

"No, sweetie, there was no way we could have predicted this," she assured Hailey as they held onto one another.

"The son of a bitch flew in on our same damn flight," Luke said when he returned. "He was on our plane." He practically growled it. "How the hell did he get on a plane?" He sat down and pulled Amber into his arms. "Hailey, this isn't on you. It's on all the idiots that let that man on a plane. All the idiots who let him fly to Vegas. The damned fool who gave him a goddamn gun while he was on a convicted felon list," he barked. "Not you. Never you."

It took almost three hours for a doctor to come out and tell them that Reece had been moved out of surgery to recovery.

It wasn't until the three of them rode the elevators up to the ICU that Hailey realized this was the first time that she had ever stepped foot in a hospital.

There were so many firsts during this trip. So many good ones followed by this one very terrible first.

More than anything, she wanted many more firsts with Reece.

They were shown into a small waiting room that was empty except for them. Here, Luke and Amber continued to take many calls and make some to fill Hannah and other family members in on Reece's status.

She'd put her phone on mute during the fight and when she pulled it out, she realized she had more than a hundred missed calls and text messages.

Seeing her sister's number, she called it.

"You're okay?" Harper said quickly when she answered.

"I am." She closed her eyes and rested her head back. "Reece." Her voice broke.

"I know, I'm here with Nick. We've been filled in on everything. Even the attack before the fight. You should have called. There, I said it and it's over. Now, how are you holding up?"

"I know, I was in shock, I think. I… didn't want to upset Reece's fight. I was going to tell you after…"

"I know," Harper said softly. "We've got him now, Fred. He's in Vegas. He won't be able to fly anywhere now."

Hailey felt a slight sense of relief.

"How's Reece? The last news we had is he's still in ICU."

"Yes, his mother is back seeing him now. They're going to move him to a private room soon, and I can see him then."

"Honey, I'm so sorry. He's strong though."

"I know," Hailey agreed. "I love him," she said softly, so quietly that Luke wouldn't hear as he talked on the phone across the room from her.

"I know. We all do," Harper said with a sigh. "I wish I was there."

"No." Hailey thought of Harper and the baby she was carrying being in the same state as Fred. She was glad Fred had gone after her instead of Harper this time.

Still, the man had to be crazy to shoot Reece in a crowded arena.

Hailey told Harper exactly what Fred had said to her after her sister put her phone on speaker so that Nick could take it down in the file they had on the man.

"What can the Las Vegas police do?" she asked, feeling a headache and realizing it was past three in the morning.

"First off, you may not have noticed but there are two officers stationed outside your waiting area to protect you," Nick answered.

Hailey glanced up and saw the two uniformed men watching the hallway. She'd just thought they worked in the hospital.

"Second, there are two outside of Reece's room. Until Fred is caught, they won't leave his or your side."

She nodded and swallowed back tears of gratitude.

"We've got you covered. When you're ready to head back to your hotel—and we've been told you can extend your reservation for the next week, if you want—someone will be with you every step of the way," Nick assured her.

"Thanks," she said, her voice cracking.

"Try and find a place to get some sleep," Harper said.

She wanted to tell her sister that there was no way she was going to sleep until after she saw Reece and made sure that he was okay. She needed to see it for herself.

Instead, she said her goodbyes and hung up.

"We can go in now," Luke said when she got off the phone. "They've moved him to a private room." He helped her stand up.

She followed him like a zombie down the hallway, too blinded by her tears to focus on where they were going. When they stepped into a dark room, Amber was there, sitting next to a bed.

She wiped her eyes clear and looked at Reece lying in the bed, and broke down again. There were tubes sticking out of his arms and chest. He was pale. His hair was sticking up all over the place.

He looked...

For the first time since she'd met him, he looked fragile.

She rushed to the side of the bed and took his hand in hers, only to realize there were tubes sticking out of it. Afraid that she'd hurt him, she tucked her hands under her armpits.

"Is... is he awake?" she asked Amber.

"He comes and goes. He's been asking for you though," Amber said softly. Then she looked over Hailey's shoulder and nodded. "I think now that we know he's out of the worst of it, we're going to go get a few hours of sleep. They retrieved my purse, and I have my phone again. We've arranged it so you can stay here for now. Get some rest." She motioned to the chair. "It folds out into a bed. A nurse will help you. I'll bring you a change of clothes in the morning, if you want."

She nodded, not taking her eyes from Reece.

"Here's the hotel key." She pulled it out of her purse and handed it to Reece's mother. "You can bring my entire bag, everything's in there. Reece's too, if you want. I don't think I'll be leaving here until he does."

Amber nodded and then hugged her. "Take care of him. Let us know if anything changes. We'll be back in a few hours."

When they were alone in the room, Hailey moved over to sit in the chair Amber had just been in and took Reece's hand, the one that was free of tubes.

"I'm here," she told him, her voice sounding odd in the silence of the room.

Tears rolled down her cheeks freely as she waited in the dark, counting the blips on the heart monitor screen and watching his closed eyelids in hopes that they would open.

When the sun started streaming in the windows behind her, she spared a glance outside. The Nevada sun assured her it was going to be another warm day outside.

Nurses had come and gone many times in the night, each one trying to strike up a conversation with her.

She politely answered their questions but remained silent as much as she could. Her eyes hardly ever left Reece's face.

When his parents appeared again a few hours after the sun had come up, her stomach was growling loudly and she was in desperate need of a bathroom break and some coffee if she was going to stay awake any longer.

"Here," Amber said. "We got everything out of your rooms." She rolled Hailey's bag in and set it next to the bathroom. "Take some time, clean up. Luke is going to head down to the cafeteria and get us some coffee and food. I'll sit with him until you come back."

When Hailey stood up, she wobbled slightly, and Amber rushed over and took her arms.

"Have you stood up once since we left?" Amber asked.

Hailey shook her head. "I didn't need to." She felt all the blood rush to her legs. "I'll be just a few minutes." She rolled her bag into the bathroom.

She quickly showered, pulled her hair up into a messy bun, and put on a pair of jeans and a fresh shirt. When she stepped out less than half an hour later, Luke was there with breakfast.

To her surprise, the moment she stepped out of the bathroom, Reece's eyes flew open.

"Hailey!" he shouted, and tried to sit up.

Chapter Twenty

What a terrible dream. Reece's mind circled over and over the past evening's events until all he could think about was getting to Hailey. Seeing her face one more time.

When he woke, her name was the only thing that came out.

Even when he was held down, he shouted for her.

"I'm here," she said, suddenly appearing in front of him. "Reece, you have to be still now."

He blinked and, seeing her face, completely relaxed his body.

"You're here." He reached for her.

She moved closer and touched his face. "I'm here," she said again. "Please, you're going to hurt yourself."

"Are you okay?" His words came out like he was drunk, slurred and all running together.

"I'm okay," she said softly. "I'm here."

She leaned down and brushed her lips across his and he settled down. This was right. This was home.

He slept for a while again and, this time when he woke up, pain shot through his chest and his arms and legs.

He must have groaned because his mother's face appeared followed by Hailey's.

"Are you in pain?" his mother asked. "I'll hit the button and get you more medicine." He heard a beep and felt the warm fluid enter the veins in his arm. For now, he wasn't going to deny himself relief from the sharp pain. He knew that the more the medicine wore off, the worse it would be.

"What happened?" he asked, wanting to cough, but afraid it would hurt even more.

"You were shot," his mother answered after a pause.

He frowned. He remembered that part.

"No, I mean, did I win?" he asked.

After another pause, his mother chuckled. "Yes, son, you did win the fight."

"You remember getting shot?" Hailey asked him. "But not if you won the fight?"

He glanced over at her and smiled. "It's kind of a blur." He assessed his body and realized that most of it was still numb, all except a few ribs and a spot close to his right shoulder. "How many times did the bastard get me?"

"Twice," his mother answered.

"You... you know it was Fred?" Hailey asked.

He did now. He'd only been talking about whoever had pulled the trigger.

"Shit, it was that asshat?" He winced when his mother made a noise at his language. "Sorry, Mom."

"It's okay. Any man who shoots my son *is* an asshat," his mother replied quickly. "I'm going to get your father. He is just down the hall to get some drinks."

"Hey, Hailey," he said, and she appeared over him again. He determined that his right arm was free of tubes and reached up to cup her face. He pulled her down until their lips were inches apart. "I love you."

He saw her eyes soften. Tears filled them. He felt them drop on his face as she brushed her lips across his.

"I love you too," she said softly.

"I was going to tell you after the fight," he admitted.

She was quiet. "It's my fault," she said, leaning back.

"What? Me falling in love with you? It sure is." He smiled, feeling a little dizzy now that the meds had hit his system.

She shook her head. "Fred attacked me before the fight. Your mother—"

"What?" He jerked a little and instantly regretted the move.

"Your mother and I fought him off and escaped. Security was looking for him, and we figured it was best if we didn't distract you before the fight."

"Did he hurt you?" he asked, glancing around to ask his mother the same.

"No, I was fighting him off, using the moves you'd shown me, when your mother did an amazing flying tackle and took him down. We ran away and he escaped out the fire door."

He remembered hearing the alarms going off in his room just before he'd left to head into the arena. He was told that some idiot had opened the fire door and it was nothing.

"How did he get back in with a gun?" he asked.

"That's still under investigation," his father said when he stepped into the room. "How are you feeling, son?"

"The drugs are making everything fuzzy. I don't know if I'll be awake in five minutes, so hurry up and tell me they've caught the asshat."

His father's face told him that no, they hadn't caught Fred yet.

"Shit," he said, feeling himself slip further into a drugged state. "Mom, are you okay?" he asked, his words slurring again.

"I'm fine, son. Get some rest. We will keep an eye on Hailey and you until you're awake." She leaned down and placed a kiss on his forehead as he once again faded into the darkness.

"You're only doing this for attention," his sister's voice woke him the next time. "See, I was right," Hannah said, her nose inches from his own. "Hey, stupid."

He smiled. "Hi, ugly."

Hannah smiled. "I heard you went and won a fight and then to celebrate, you got shot."

He groaned. "At least I won."

"Yes, you did. Stupid." Hannah leaned down and kissed him on the forehead where his mother had.

"Where is everyone?" he asked when he realized that the room was quiet.

"Sleeping. It's three in the morning. We finally convinced Hailey to go back to a hotel room and get some real sleep."

"What day is it?" he asked, feeling fully awake for some reason.

"Three days after you got shot," Hannah answered, leaning back in her chair. I flew out here earlier. Mom and Dad were worn out, and Hailey..." She shook her head.

Worry flooded him. "What's wrong with Hailey?" he asked, wishing he could sit up more.

"She's exhausted. She hadn't left your side for more than a few minutes to go to the bathroom or shower. It took a call from her sister to finally convince her to go back with the folks and get some real rest." Hannah took his hand in hers. "How are you feeling?"

"The sharp pain in my chest is now dull. It might be due to the drugs, but it's not as bad as it was the last time I woke up."

"Rest," Hannah said with a smile. "Your body is healing quickly. You'll be up and punching more grown men in underwear soon enough."

He shook his head. "No, I think I'm done with that career. Nothing can top the other night." He smiled. "You know what they say, quit while you're ahead."

Hannah smiled at him. "Good, because we like your face the way it is."

"Have they caught Fred yet?"

Hannah shook her head. "Not yet."

He was quiet for a moment. "When can I go home?"

"If they can get you on your feet and walking around, a day or two," Hannah said.

"Any permanent damage?"

Hannah shook her head. "Skin, muscles, and a broken rib or two." She sighed. "You were extremely lucky."

He agreed as he thought of the other possibilities.

"Do the police have any clue where the man is?" he asked.

"No, but they're not taking any chances. Nick and Tom have arranged for a twenty-four hour watch on Hailey and you until you return home," Hannah said.

"Yeah, I remember dad mentioning that before I blacked out again."

"They moved to the hotel across the street. They can be here in a few minutes if you want?" Hannah asked.

"No, I'm okay. Is there a television in here?" he asked. "I'm wide awake."

"Sure, here." Hannah handed him a remote. "I'm awake too. I slept on the plane and had a nice long nap before you woke up."

After flipping through the many home shopping channels, he finally found a news station. His sister shifted over and sat next to him on the bed.

Even though he had a dull ache in his side, he allowed her to snuggle up against him like the old days when they were kids.

They watched the news in silence, and when a report about the fight came on, he smiled as he watched the replay of him taking down Carrigan.

"Everyone stood over you," Hannah said softly. "Even Carrigan." She pointed and, sure enough, Reece could see the man locking arms with the others to protect Reece while his parents, and Hailey knelt beside him.

"She loves me," he admitted to Hannah.

"Duh," Hannah said, nudging his leg. "I think the entire world knows that now."

He smiled. "Do you think she'll marry me?"

"You?" Hannah looked at him and squished up her face. "You're too stupid for that."

He laughed. "Wyatt is marrying you."

"He's smart," she countered.

"So is Hailey," he pointed out, and his sister's smile grew.

"Yes, she is. Yes, baby brother, I think you found someone smart enough to marry you." She leaned up and kissed his cheek.

Two days later, he slowly made his way up his front stairs. Ali was staying at his sister's place for now until he was a little steadier on his feet.

"I'll take your bags upstairs," his father called out halfway up the stairs.

"The meal train dropped off enough meals to fill your freezer," his mother said as they made their way to his sofa.

"Thanks." He sat down, feeling completely drained from the flight and drive home.

He patted the spot on the sofa next to him for Hailey to sit down as his mother made her way back to the kitchen, no doubt to check that everything had been delivered and put away.

"How does it feel to be home?" she asked him with a smile.

"Good, how do you feel?" he replied.

"Tired," she admitted. "I could sleep for a week."

He nodded. "My folks will leave, and we can snuggle here on the sofa. I'm too tired to head up those stairs at the moment."

"Everything's in place. The hospital's instructions and your medicines are on the kitchen counter." His mother walked over and kissed him on the forehead. "Get some rest. Both of you." She motioned towards them just as his father came down the stairs.

"Let us know if you need anything," his dad added.

"Thanks," Hailey called after them as they walked out. He heard the front door lock engage and then kicked off his shoes and pulled Hailey down onto the sofa until they were snuggled tight together. It didn't even hurt his chest.

"See, much better," he assured her.

"The remote is over there," Hailey said with a chuckle.

He groaned and then released her so she could grab it and a blanket to cover them both.

Then, to his happy surprise, she lifted her shirt slightly

and removed her bra in several moves without taking her shirt off. They she lay back down in front of him.

"Later, when I have enough energy to do something about it, I'm going to want to see that show again," he told her, causing her to chuckle.

"Tell me again," he said, as she flipped through the channels to find a movie for them to watch.

She giggled. "I love you."

"I love you," he said, and before she could even start a movie, he fell asleep with the smell of her hair filling his mind.

He woke to the smell of food. Well, to be exact, his stomach woke him. The loud growl almost echoed in the house.

The television was still on but muted.

He sat up and rubbed his hands over his face, thankful the pain was bearable.

"How are you feeling?" Hailey asked, walking into the room with a tray of food.

"Rested. The pain is low enough that I'm going to try and skip the evening pills," he said when she set the tray down and he saw the pills on it.

She frowned at him.

"How about we cut them in half?" She took one pill and held it out to him. "I'm afraid you're going to be hurting too much later to head down here and take another one in the middle of the night."

He agreed and swallowed the pill.

"What's for dinner?" he asked.

"Chicken casserole." She sat next to him.

"Lacey Jordan's," he said after taking a bite.

She laughed. "I'll bet you can tell me who made every dish in your freezer by taste."

"Yeah, I probably could," he admitted as he took another bite.

They ate in silence for a while.

"I have to work tomorrow," she said with a sigh. "I'm looking forward to going back, but if you need me..."

"We've talked about this. I'm good." He shifted and only winced slightly. "It's been a week."

"Only a week," she countered.

"I'm good," he said again. "Go to work. My sister and parents will, no doubt, be by here again tomorrow to check up on me."

She nodded. "Nick thinks that he is still in Vegas."

Reece didn't want to worry her so he just nodded. There were other ways to leave a state.

"They're going to have someone looking out for both you and Harper. Don't worry, the entire town is watching out as well." He lifted his arm slowly and put it around her.

"It's on the news again." Hailey motioned to the screen.

This time, the report showed the image of Fred that Harper had taken at the cabin along with a new one from the hotel's surveillance cameras. There were grainy images of Fred attacking Hailey and of Amber coming to her rescue.

He wished there were videos of his mother's flying tackle, but apparently there were only photos in the hallway where they had been attacked.

The man's photo was on every channel. Every police officer from Nevada to Oregon was on the lookout for the man.

This time there was another report of how Fred Leeroy had gotten the gun. They'd heard all about the stolen weapon taken from the hotel room next to his, which he'd paid cash for. The clerk had called the police immediately when they had released his name and photos.

"Do you think they will ever find him?" Hailey asked, sounding tired again.

"Without a doubt," he answered quickly, pulling her into his arms. "Without a doubt."

He felt her relax against him. "When?"

"Soon. Until then, we'll be extra careful. Like we talked about." He kissed the top of her head as she nodded in agreement.

"No one is left alone," she repeated.

He smiled. "Now, since I know this town and its people so well, I can guarantee that there are no fewer than three pies in the kitchen. How about we take a few pieces upstairs?"

She laughed and nodded. "There are four. What flavor? Chocolate, cherry, apple, and blueberry."

He smiled. "Megan Jordan's apple pie is the best."

Chapter Twenty-One

Hailey was very thankful for work the next day. Even more thankful for the people in Pride when she was greeted with hugs and well wishes.

She was home. She had finally found a place that she would fight to stay in. She knew that Harper felt the same way.

Not only were Reece's freezer and refrigerator filled with enough food to feed an army, but the cupboards were also packed with canned food as well.

And Corey and Carter had gone out of their way to accommodate her hours so she could make up her missed time if she wanted to.

At first, she was worried that she would miss the extra money in her bank account, but then Reece reminded her of the nine hundred dollars that she'd won in Vegas before the fight, so she wasn't too concerned about catching up on her hours.

What mattered most to her was helping Reece get back in shape.

Sometime before dinner, Harper and Nick strolled into Baked.

She hugged her sister and took her break to eat dinner with them.

"I stopped by Reece's place before I got off shift and filled him in on the hunt. Fred was spotted at a gas station just outside of Reno. He purchased a truck with cash just outside of Vegas."

"Reno?" Hailey frowned. "Does that mean he's heading back here?"

"No," Nick answered quickly. "What it means is we have the make, model, and license plate of the vehicle and have all states looking out for him. He won't get a chance to get back in the state."

Hailey tried to relax, but Reno was only a ten-hour drive or so from Pride. The man had made it halfway back to town before being spotted.

After her sister and Nick left, she tried to keep her spirits up. Tried to stay focused on work. In the end, she left work with a slight headache and a stomachache from only having half a slice of pizza during dinner.

The moment she stepped into the house, Reece was there to greet her. Seeing her face, he wrapped his arms around her and held on.

"What's wrong?" he asked after a moment.

"He's made it to Reno already," she said with a sniffle.

Reece sighed. "Yeah. But think of this as a good thing. We know where he's going. Did you ever watch *Scooby Doo*?"

She frowned and leaned back. "The cartoon?"

He nodded and smiled at her as he took her hand and walked slowly into the kitchen. "It's time we lay a trap."

She rolled her eyes. "This is real life."

"So do you think the man is smart enough to know that we'd lay a trap for him?" he asked her.

"I don't think Fred is smart at all. After all, he shot at you and tried to kidnap me in the middle of a crowded hotel," she pointed out.

Reece nodded. "Nick and I have a few ideas."

"Such as?" she asked, sitting down at the bar.

"Let's heat up one of these meals and I'll go over them with you."

Once they had heated up a massive pan of shepherd's pie, which apparently was made by Iian Jordan, and were sitting at the kitchen table, Reece ran through a few ideas.

All of them use Nick or Reece as bait.

"This is stupid." She set her fork down. "Fred isn't after you or Nick. He would hurt you to get to us. But I don't think he'd hunt you down."

"He will when—" Reece started, but she held up her hand to stop him.

"He doesn't care if you call him out," Hailey said, rubbing her forehead.

"What does he care about?" Reece asked as they ate their dessert.

"Me," she admitted, looking down at her plate. "He called me his princess." She shivered. Suddenly, Reece's arms were around her. "For some crazy reason, he wants me. He wants Harper to suffer. To die." She shivered again.

"I won't chance you being the bait," he said into her hair.

"Then we'll live in fear until he's caught."

They held one another for a while. "How about a bath?" he asked her. "I can't shower, but maybe if I'm careful, I can sit across a bath from you."

She smiled. "We can try. Just as long as there are bubbles."

He laughed. "I haven't had a bubble bath since I was five. My mother and sister were in charge back then." He kissed her. "Now you're in charge."

The bath was huge and took a long time to fill up with water and bubbles. And since Reece still had bandages on both of his wounds, he could only put his legs and feet in the water and was wearing his boxer briefs still. Sitting in the bubble bath with Reece across from her somehow made her feel like a kid.

"Here." He shifted and slowly made his way around the tub until he sat directly behind her. "Lean back."

She leaned back against his legs and instantly felt more relaxed than before. Reece started rubbing her head, and she remembered the massages they'd had in Vegas.

That day seemed like years ago now.

"The only thing that will assure that Harper and her and Nick's baby are safe is if I put myself out there in the line of danger." She opened her eyes. "I have to be the bait."

He closed his eyes and sighed. "I'll run the idea by Nick. Tomorrow."

"Reece." She flipped around until she was kneeling in front of him. "Whatever happens, I want to be with you. No matter what."

His smile returned. "I'm not going to let you go."

She smiled. "You're mine. Fred knew that. That's why he went after you."

"I'm just thankful he waited until after I won." Reece ran his hands down her wet hair. "Even though my career is over, I'm thankful I had a few seconds in the spotlight."

Her heart ached each time she thought of the fact that

Reece would never box professionally again. And due to his injuries, maybe not even as just a pass time.

The media was calling him a legend. The boxer who could have been great. Like the movie stars that were killed in their youth and had become greats even if their acting was below par.

Reece Crawford would be one of those greats in the boxing world, right up there with William Billy Cox, his idol.

"You know, we never did get to celebrate your big win," she said, changing tactics as her hands started running up his legs.

His eyebrows shot up. "Oh, what did you have in mind. Remember, I'm still recovering."

"I think I can find something that will please us both." She slipped her hand up his boxers and found him hard already.

"I have a confession. I really like watching you bathe," he said with a chuckle.

"Good." She shifted closer and started pulling his boxers off. He held his legs up to help her, and she pulled them off and tossed them aside.

"This"—she took him in her hands—"is something I thought I'd never have."

"My cock?" he asked in a low tone. "Cuz you can have it anytime you want."

She laughed. "No, desire. Want." She leaned in and ran her tongue over him before taking him fully into her mouth.

She had no clue what she was doing, but figured she'd try a few things. Each time he groaned with pleasure, she continued to explore him.

"Hailey, you're going to make me come," he warned.

"Good," she said softly.

"Are you sure?" he asked her.

She glanced up, meeting his eyes. "Yes." She returned to pleasing him.

Feeling his warmth fill her mouth seconds later, she knew that she would always trust him. There was nothing Reece could ever do to scare her.

This was the man of her dreams. The man she wanted to spend the rest of her life with.

The man she wanted to love forever.

The next morning, she woke in the bed alone. She could see the gray sky outside and knew that it was raining again.

One thing she loved about living in Oregon was the weather. Most people didn't like rain. Hailey loved it. Today was going to be one of those days where they wouldn't ever see the sun, and she was actually happy about it.

She could hear Reece talking, and she pulled on a robe and found him on the phone in the bathroom.

"It's Nick," he said with a sigh. "I was hoping not to wake you. Nick, I've got you on speaker. Hailey's awake."

"Good, so, I'll repeat what I just told Reece. We found the truck Fred was driving. It was abandoned along Highway One ten miles out of town."

"He's here." Hailey felt tingles race all over her body. "Harper?"

"Is staying at my parents' place for the time being," Nick responded. "Fred has no clue who or where they are."

Hailey relaxed and sat on the edge of the tub.

"I don't really like the idea of using you as bait," Nick continued. "I'd like a day to see if we can smoke him out. From what Harper has said, he's pretty comfortable in the woods. The picture she took of him, he was wearing hiking and camping gear. We know that when he was in town before, he didn't stay at the hotel except for a few nights. We think he camped out by the cabin."

"Do you think he's at the cabin again?" Hailey asked.

"We're going to go check it out later this morning. Whatever we do, I don't think we will spook him into acting until he can get a hold of either of you. We know he probably still has the gun he used on Reece. I've asked the state PD to lend a hand, and they're sending some men to help in the search. For now, the two of you are to stay put today."

"I have work," Hailey started.

"Not today. Call in sick. Corey and Carter will understand," Nick added.

She nodded and looked to Reece.

"We're sticking here," Reece confirmed. "Keep us in the loop."

"Will do," Nick said before hanging up.

"I'm going to go call Carter." She got up.

"I'll head downstairs and make us some breakfast." Reece kissed her. "My sister is going to bring Ali home later today." He smiled. "I miss the guy."

"Me too," she admitted as she called Carter.

Carter, as she had expected, totally understood, and told her that if she needed anything to let them know.

"Take your time coming back. However long you need, take it," he added before hanging up.

She took a moment to pull on a pair of sweats and one of Reece's T-shirts before heading downstairs.

"Hey, I don't smell any coffee," she called out when she hit the bottom of the stairs.

She frowned when Reece didn't respond right away. Had he fallen? Somehow hurt himself?

Then she stepped into the kitchen and froze. There was

a trail of blood leading from the kitchen island to the back hallway towards the mud room.

She raced through the kitchen, following it to the back door in the mud room. There, taped to the broken glass of the back door, was a note.

She ripped it down with shaky fingers.

"You know where to find me, Princess. Come alone or you won't even get to say goodbye."

Everything in her body froze. The tingle on her skin was back, causing her to shiver.

Reaching for the hook by the back door where they hung the car keys, she realized Reece's keys were gone. Looking out, she knew why. His truck was gone too.

She took her keys and grabbed her coat off the hook in the mud room. She shoved her cell phone into her pocket.

She ran to her truck in the rain, praying with each step she took.

Thoughts of calling Nick were pushed out of her mind quickly. There was no way she was going to chance Reece's life. Not when she'd just gotten him back.

The amount of blood on the kitchen floor worried her as she drove towards the cabin. Had he attacked Reece?

She knew that the only way Reece would have gone with the man is if he was unconscious. There was no way Fred would kill him. Yet.

Panic threatened to take over, causing her to swerve and almost drive off the road. Her wipers were working fast to clear the rain from her vision.

What was she going to do? How could she save Reece?

Why did Fred take Reece away from the house and drag him to the cabin? Why not knock Reece out and head upstairs? She'd been there, alone.

Then she remembered how Fred had always enjoyed ruining or destroying anything she and Harper loved.

One day they had come home to find a small fort they'd built destroyed. He'd laughed and laughed when they'd cried over it.

He knew how much the sisters loved the cabin. How much hard work they'd done. He'd hurt them when he'd destroying the bathroom tiles.

Was he planning on destroying the cabin?

Or on killing Reece there to forever taint the location for her?

Oh god!

Then she remembered Nick's conversation. They were going to stop by the cabin this morning. There was a chance he and Tom were there already. Would they see Reece's truck? Would they know what was going on or would Fred freak out upon seeing the police there and kill Reece before she had a chance to get there, to say goodbye to him.

She slammed her foot down on the pedal and prayed as she drove faster.

Two minutes. She was two minutes away from the cabin.

Just hold on. She sent up a prayer. Just hold on.

Chapter Twenty-Two

What in the hell?

Reece woke with a splitting headache. Where was he?

He stilled and listened. He was in a car.

He frowned and then felt the rain hitting his face and looked around. His vision was a little blurry but it only took a moment for him to realize that he was in the back of his truck.

Why?

Then he remembered.

He'd stepped into the kitchen to make them some coffee. He'd stilled when a gun was shoved into his side.

"You're one tough son of a bitch," someone had said behind him just before pain exploded on the side of his head above his left ear and everything went black.

Shit. He'd been kidnapped.

He was freaking Daphne from *Scooby Doo*. A fucking damsel in distress.

He was about to jump out of the truck when it came to a skidding halt.

"Not so fast." Fred jumped out of the truck, the gun aimed at Reece's chest. "I doubt you can recover from a bullet at this range."

"Why? What the fuck do you want with Hailey?" He practically screamed it.

Fred's wicked smile answered the question.

"Did you know she was pure when I had her? Harper too, the first time." He chuckled. "I used to like 'em young. It was easy, finding a mark with young kids. Selling drugs was just an easy way of getting my foot in the door, getting what I wanted." He motioned with the gun. "Inside, let's get out of the rain while we wait for my princess."

"She won't come here," Reece said, slowly getting out of the back of the truck.

"Oh, I think she will. Everyone knows how she feels about you." Fred shoved the gun in Reece's side. Thankfully, it was the side that didn't have broken ribs that were healing.

Reece knew all the moves to escape the situation. Moves that didn't involve a gun being shoved in his side.

Until he could find the perfect time, the only thing he could do was go along with it and pray that Hailey wouldn't show up.

"Why give up so much to come across the country for them?" he asked as Fred kicked open the cabin door as if it was made of cardboard. He shoved Reece inside.

There was a fire burning in the fireplace. Fred must have spent the night there and wanted to keep the place warm. It was just embers at this point, but the fire had done its job. The house was nice and cozy.

"Give up?" Fred laughed. "My business was going under. I sank all the money I made off their whore mother into that club. The Atlanta PD are eyeing me for a few other bitch druggies that OD'd. Their bitch daughters are crying rape and the cops are asking a lot of questions. Even some of my workers are lying about how young they were when I hired 'em." Fred forced him to sit down on Harper and Hailey's sofa. It was obvious now that the man had spent the night there. He was very comfortable with the space, as if he owned it.

"So, you what? Leave everything for a chance with Harper and Hailey again?" he asked, knowing he had to keep the man talking.

It was only a matter of time before Nick and Tom would swing by the cabin. No doubt, they'd see his truck parked out front and know something was wrong.

After all, he'd just gotten off the phone with Nick minutes ago and promised that he and Hailey would stay at his place all day.

"If you have to go, might as well take someone with you," Fred said with a smile. "Besides, I'd like a taste of that sweet nectar again. I only had her once, but she was the sweetest thing I've ever had. I've been trying to find someone else like her." He shook his head. "Nothing compares. Not even close."

"If you lay a hand on her..." He dropped off when the gun moved to the center of his head.

"You're just lucky I don't pull this trigger right now," Fred warned in a low voice. He was silent for a moment before shifting the gun lower again. "I watched you fight. Rooted for the other guy to knock all your teeth out." He smiled. "Impressive. I could still kick your ass." His eyes ran over Reece. "Course, you're in bad shape now, it wouldn't be a fair fight." He laughed. "Still, I might have some fun before my princess gets here." He lifted the gun as if to swing out and hit Reece again but at that moment, they both heard a car turn up the gravel driveway.

When Fred's head jerked towards the sound, Reece took his opportunity and kicked out.

His foot connected with the gun just as Fred jerked back and pulled the trigger. The gun flew out of Fred's hand and landed a foot from the fireplace.

Reece rushed the man, shoving his body as hard as he could back away from the door where he worried that Hailey would come rushing in at any moment.

On a good day, he could have easily taken the man, even though he outweighed him. Now, however, with his body weakened by the trauma, he struggled just to keep a hold on him and keep him from grabbing the gun and shooting him again.

In the battle that followed, they knocked over several pieces of furniture. Fred threw one of the logs from the fireplace at him, but he missed and the log fell to the floor, where it instantly caught the rug and curtains on fire.

Reece threw his entire weight at the man, and the duo rolled around on the hardwood floor.

He managed to get his legs wrapped around the man's chest while his arms strained to hold his neck. He had him locked in the hold for a split second before he took an elbow to his broken ribs and lost his hold altogether.

He ended up in a heap on the floor, gasping for breath as Fred stood over him, the gun aimed at his head.

Reece glanced up, looking death directly in the eyes. He watched Fred's fingers slowly move towards the trigger. Seconds ticked by. Fred smiled and laughed, then he stopped as the point of a fireplace poker was jammed into the side of his head.

Fred's eyes rolled backwards. He fell to his knees as

blood spurt out of the deep wound where the poker stuck out of his head. The man crumpled at his feet without another sound.

When the man landed, Hailey rushed over and wrapped her arms around him.

"Are you okay?" she asked, gasping.

"Out," he managed to say between deep breaths.

Hailey helped him stand up and the pair rushed out the front door into the rain just as the sofa caught fire.

"Reece, are you okay?" she asked when he collapsed a few feet outside of the door.

"Call, police," he managed to say between gasps of air as he held his ribs.

"I already did. When I pulled up." She held up her phone, and he could hear Nick screaming at them.

"We're here," Hailey said. "Hurry, the cabin is on fire. I think I killed Fred," she admitted as she looked at him.

Reece nodded in agreement. Yeah, the man was gone all right.

Thankfully.

"Hold on," Hailey said. She turned the phone on speaker. "Tell him."

"We're coming up the drive now. Get away from the cabin."

Reece nodded again. Shit. He was not going to pass out. Not now. He concentrated on slowing his breathing. Regulating how much air got into his lungs and pushed out his re-broken ribs.

"I'm here." Hailey knelt in front of him as the patrol car stopped behind his truck. "Breathe," she said, calmly.

He nodded and closed his eyes and tried to focus.

"Sorry," he managed before everything turned gray.

"No, you don't," Nick said firmly as something foul was shoved in his face. "Wake up."

"Shit." He groaned. "Broken." He held his side.

"Yeah, Dr. Stevens is on his way here. My dad and his crew are as well to put out this fire." He motioned to the cabin. "From the way it's going up, I'd say that they won't be able to save it," Nick said to Hailey.

"It doesn't matter," she said, keeping her eyes on Reece. "I have everything I want right here."

She held onto him lightly, and he struggled to stand up so they could step away from the growing heat.

"I moved your truck back. The keys were still inside," Tom said, stopping beside him.

"Thanks," he managed.

They turned as the fire truck came up the driveway.

Watching the cabin, the first home that Hailey and Harper had ever had, burn to the ground, saddened him. Knowing that Fred was inside relieved him.

"It's done," Hailey said with a sigh.

No matter how much the firemen fought to save the cabin, there was nothing they could do. Even the heavy rain falling over them did little to stop the old wood home from going up.

By the time Harper and Nick's mother showed up, there was nothing left but embers.

Harper ran to Hailey and hugged her.

"It's gone," Hailey cried.

"It doesn't matter," Harper said over and over. "Only you and Reece matter." She smiled at him.

Doctor Stevens was there. He'd patched the cut on the back of Reece's head and was trying to convince him to go to Edgeview and get more X-rays of his ribs. But in truth, now that he had his breathing under control, the pain had lightened up.

He promised the doctor that he'd go in the next day and get checked out. Right now, however, he was where he was needed most.

When there was nothing left of the cabin, he climbed into Hailey's truck and let her drive him home. Nick was going to drive his truck back to the house later once he was done securing the site.

Harper followed them and while they waited for Nick, they sat in his kitchen.

When Hailey stepped into the house, she rushed to clean up the blood before his parents, Nick's mother, and Hannah and Wyatt arrived.

Within the hour, his house was full of family and friends.

The entire town knew about the fire, knew about what Hailey had done to save his life. And no one called her a murder. Not one person condemned her for her actions.

Everyone, however, was sad that the sisters had lost their home.

Food was brought and shared. A plate of chicken and mashed potatoes was shoved in front of his face, and he realized that it was after noon. The entire morning was gone.

Hailey never left his side. She ate quietly as she listened to his sister fill them in on Ali's shenanigans, as she called them.

His dog, or rather, *their* dog had apparently been very mischievous while staying at his auntie Hannah's house.

"You should have called him mayhem instead of Ali," Hannah joked.

"Thank you," he said, taking his sister's hand in his.

"Any time. Ali and Luna are best friends now." Hannah

sighed. "We're going to have to let the four siblings have playdates regularly," she said to Harper.

"Any time." Harper smiled.

Just then, Nick walked in the kitchen and walked over to place a kiss on Harper's lips.

"Is he...?" Hailey said, dropping off.

Nick nodded. "We found him just where you said he was."

Hailey leaned back and then Harper hugged her sister. "It's over," she said into Hailey's hair.

He thought of telling Nick what the man had said before he'd fought him. Whatever happened, he knew that he shouldn't do it in front of the sisters. They'd gone through enough.

What he did want was closure for all the other Haileys and Harpers that Fred had terrorized. Justice. They deserved it. How many other women were out there that did too?

"Got a moment?" he said to Nick, and stood up.

Nick followed him out into the front foyer, where he filled him in on what Fred had confessed to him.

Nick took some notes down and assured him that he would work with the Atlanta PD to close any cases they had on Fred and let the victims know the man's fate.

"What will happen to Hailey?" he asked softly.

"Nothing," Nick assured him. "I know she's probably worried about that, but assure her nothing is going to happen. She stood her ground. Saved you in the process." Nick slapped him on the shoulder. "And we're thankful for it."

It was almost two hours before their house was quiet again. His father came and patched up the back door glass and warned him that it was past time he installed a security system.

Thankfully, Josh and Carrie Williams were in attendance and he hired the man on the spot to install a system as soon as possible.

When Hailey, Ali, and he climbed the stairs to head to bed, he stopped her on the landing and pulled her into his arms.

"Today was... Well, I have mixed feelings about it." He sighed.

"I'm relieved," she said, cupping his face. "Happy that he's no longer a threat. Sad that he hurt you." She touched his head softly. "Angry that Harper and I lost the first real home we ever had."

He nodded. "Yes, all of those feelings." Then he took her hand and lifted it to his lips, unknowingly brushing his mouth across her ring finger. "I'm too tired and in too much pain to do this properly, so I'll ask for a redo later, when I feel better and after about a week of sleep." He glanced into her eyes. "Marry me, Hailey. Make this our home. Fill it with love, dogs, children, and happiness. I don't want to spend a night without you in my arms. A moment without you in my life. Be mine, forever, my love. Please."

She smiled and brushed her lips across his. "Forever. I like the sound of that." She kissed him again.

Also by Jill Sanders

The Pride Series

Finding Pride

Discovering Pride

Returning Pride

Lasting Pride

Serving Pride

Red Hot Christmas

My Sweet Valentine

Return To Me

Rescue Me

A Pride Christmas

The Secret Series

Secret Seduction

Secret Pleasure

Secret Guardian

Secret Passions

Secret Identity

Secret Sauce

Secret Obsession

Secret Desire

Secret Charm

Secret Santa

The West Series

Loving Lauren

Taming Alex

Holding Haley

Missy's Moment

Breaking Travis

Roping Ryan

Wild Bride

Corey's Catch

Tessa's Turn

Saving Trace

Christmas Holly

Maggie's Match

The Grayton Series

Last Resort

Someday Beach

Rip Current

In Too Deep

Swept Away

High Tide

Sunset Dreams

Lucky Series

Unlucky In Love

Sweet Resolve

Best of Luck

A Little Luck

Christmas Wish

Silver Cove Series

Silver Lining

French Kiss

Happy Accident

Hidden Charm

A Silver Cove Christmas

Sweet Surrender

Second Chances

Dancing on Air

Entangled Series – Paranormal Romance

The Awakening

The Beckoning

The Ascension

The Presence

The Calling

The Chosen

The Beyond

The Void

Haven, Montana Series

Closer to You

Never Let Go

Holding On

Coming Home

The Hard Way

Never Again

Pride Oregon Series

A Dash of Love

My Kind of Love

Season of Love

Tis the Season

Dare to Love

Where I Belong

Because of Love

A Thing Called Love

First Comes Love

Someone to Love

Fools in Love

FindingLove

Christmas Joy

Always My Love

Forever My Love

Searching for Love

Wildflowers Series

Summer Nights

Summer Heat

Summer Secrets

Summer Fling

Summer's End

Summer Wish

Summer Breeze

Summer Ride

Distracted Series

Wake Me

Tame Me

Save Me

Dare Me

Stand Alone Books

Twisted Rock

Hope Harbor

Raven Falls

Angel Bluff

Day Break

Diamonds in the Mud

For a complete list of books:

http://JillSanders.com

About the Author

Jill Sanders is a New York Times, USA Today, and international bestselling author of Sweet Contemporary Romance, Romantic Suspense, Western Romance, and Paranormal Romance novels. With over 90 books in eleven series, translations into several different languages, and audiobooks there's plenty to choose from. Look for Jill's bestselling stories wherever romance books are sold or visit her at jillsanders.com

Jill comes from a large family with six siblings, including an identical twin. She was raised in the Pacific Northwest and later relocated to Colorado for college and a successful IT career before discovering her talent for writing sweet and sexy page-turners. After Colorado, she decided to move south, living in Texas and now making her home along the Emerald Coast of Florida. You will find that the settings of several of her series are inspired by her time spent living in these areas. She has two sons and off-set the testosterone in her house by adopting three furry little ladies that provide her company while she's locked in her writing cave. She enjoys heading to the beach, hiking, swimming, wine-tasting, and pickleball with her husband, and of course writing. If you have read any of her books, you may also notice that there is a love of food, especially sweets! She has been blamed for a few added pounds by her assistant, editor, and fans... donuts or pie anyone?

facebook.com/JillSandersBooks

x.com/JillMSanders

amazon.com/Jill-Sanders/e/B009M2NFD6?tag=jillm-com-20

bookbub.com/authors/jill-sanders

instagram.com/jillsandersauthor

tiktok.com/@jillsandersauthor

9 781945 100949